The Plastic Surgeon

AJ Carter

Dedication

For my daughter, who inspires everything I do.

And for my dog, who farts in her sleep.

The Plastic Surgeon

Prologue

THIS IS *why you should never trust anyone.*

Ten seconds ago, he was enjoying a glass of whisky, savouring the hot rush as it funnelled down his throat. It was a harsh taste but a good one. It was something he'd always looked forward to after a long day out in the sun, breaking his back with manual labour and panicking about the deadline so he could move on to the next job. That crisp flavour on his tongue was well earned, so why should tonight have been any different?

Because it was poisoned. That's why.

He knows it now. The drink had a different kick to it. Something clinical, perhaps synthetic. The burn is like nothing he's ever had before, like lava spilling into the pit of his stomach. The aftertaste is so aggressive he swears he can hear it hiss. Or maybe that's his throat, a plea for help drowned out by the gargling sound that follows.

Help, is all he tries to say.

For all the good it does. The only person in the room is the one who's done this to him. He stumbles back, reaching for his throat as if it will help. It won't – nothing will. This man is as good as dead, and he knows it.

His back strikes the wall with a violent crash. He doubles over, then begins to pace as his vision grows blurry. It's like eating the world's hottest pepper. He can't think or walk straight. As he reaches for the door handle to get far away, his hand hits flat air twice before finding purchase. Then, while he tries to make it to the end of the gravel driveway, his legs give out. The ground rushes up to meet him, but he feels nothing.

Nothing.

The fire in his belly is dying. His eyes flutter and then close. There's no way he's getting up from this – no way he will live to see another day. This is the end of his journey, and all he can think about as he lies there dying is something his father taught him.

This, *he thinks*... this is why you should never trust anyone.

Chapter 1
Daisy, Now

WE'RE all entitled to our secrets, no?

Mine are something else. Newsworthy, you might say, but that's only if it gets out. All you need to know for now is that I'm so unhappy with how I look that I feel the need for drastic change. The kind of changes that will alter my entire face.

Have I always hated my own face? Maybe I've been subtly uncomfortable with the features I was bullied for in school, but I was prepared to overlook them until recent events. I won't go into it until I'm ready, but for now, just know that I loved someone who wasn't quite sure how to be good to a woman. Because of that, my confidence is on the floor.

Because of that, I'm getting surgery today.

I meet my surgeon for the first time in the

clinic café. He's a tall guy, thin but in one of those slick, athletic ways. His jaw is so tight that I wonder if he gets a staff discount for surgeries, and his face has that sexy, pointed look to it. As if that's not enough to make me swoon, his sapphire eyes are piercing, and they pin me down with something between a smile and a bad-boy look. It's a childish desire, but it's real.

'I'm Cillian. Are you ready for your surgery?' he asks, picking apart a cheese sandwich.

I nod, standing there with my bottled water in hand and trying to get away because I'm too shy to talk to the gorgeous surgeon. Then, when it goes silent, I stumble to fill the void. 'The team are really sweet and caring. They ran me through everything that's going to happen, taking extra time to assure me everything is going to be okay.'

'Ah, you're one of the nervous ones.'

'Are there many of us?'

The surgeon – Cillian – shrugs and pops some grated cheddar into his mouth. 'Everyone is nervous on one level or another. Some more than others. But honestly, it will be fine. You'll breathe through the mask, have the best sleep of your life, then wake up and be taken back to your room for some food.'

That's exactly what the rest of the team told me in that little room where they did all the checks. It's nice to hear it again because it assures me of how painless this should be. Except for the recovery process, of course. So much is being done: rhinoplasty, chin liposuction, a chin implant, and ear pinning. I feel like I'm going into that theatre looking like one person and will be coming out looking like someone else entirely. That's a good thing.

That's where the bastard left my self-confidence.

I thank Cillian and then go sit at the table by the window. There's not much of a view, just a row of posh-looking buildings across the street. I like to watch people as they pass, wondering where they're going and what they're thinking. Have they had as hard a year as me? Have they gone through the horrors I have with someone they were supposed to be able to trust? For their sakes, I hope not. Nobody deserves to be treated that way.

This isn't the right time to be thinking about it. All I need to focus on is the surgery, and then I can get out of here with all the alterations I ever wanted. I'm not expecting the recovery process to be easy, but the sooner we get started, the sooner I can put the ugly, unlovable old Daisy in the past, and maybe – just maybe – someone can love me again.

Someday, at least.

THE BEST SLEEP of my life.

That was what Cillian promised, and he delivered. I lie awake as if in an unknown land, my head fuzzy but in a nice way. Like stepping off a massage table or feeling the first slight effects of a large glass of wine. Two nurses are at my feet, messing around with charts and mumbling something between themselves. I say something to them, but don't ask me what. I've still got one foot in dreamland, and I'm not fully invested in the real world.

As they wheel me back to the room where I'll be staying for less than twenty-four hours, I begin to recognise the bandaging around my face. That was a lot of surgery to go through in just one day, but I'm glad I did it. Like I said, I need to not look how *he* saw me.

I'm taken care of, with doctors popping into my room from time to time. I'm secretly hoping to see Cillian again – there's something charming about him that makes me feel safe and taken care of. After the relationship I've had, I could use a little safety. Sadly, he makes no such appearance. It crosses my mind that the aftercare might not be all it was sold as and that they've got the money now, so don't concern themselves too much with what happens after. Like it's all just a procedure to them. I suppose it is.

When I start to wake up a little, I send a text to my cousin Lily. And before you say anything, it's not lost on me that we're both named after flowers. We theorised that our parents (who are sisters) designed it that way so they could emphasise how cute we were. 'Aww, let's have a nice day out with Daisy and Lily,' they might say, and the other mothers around them would press a hand to their hearts.

It's enough to make you sick.

Anyway, I tell Lily that I'm out of surgery and am still ready for her to pick me up tomorrow from the clinic's front doors. It's my best version of the English language anyway. Honestly, I'm absolutely exhausted. Not the sleepy kind of tired, but just drained. Like I've been out in the sun all day, or I've just run a marathon. As soon as the text is sent, I log in to the clinic Wi-Fi and turn to the streaming services just to keep myself occupied. I'm trying to focus on an easy comedy show – I really am – but the pain is real.

Firstly, there's a big cast around my nose that I'm not allowed to take off for a whole week. It makes breathing difficult, as does the leakage seeping from it. As if that's not enough to irritate me, I've had a compression garment strapped to my head, which is stuffed with padding that has to stay on for forty-eight hours before I can quickly take it off just to shower. They did warn me in advance that the recovery was going to be painful, but I never truly thought it would be this uncomfortable. Every second wrapped up in this thing makes me feel like I'm about to suffocate. How I'm supposed to sleep like this, I'll never know.

But at least I look like a new woman.

That's all I ever wanted.

SOMEHOW, I do sleep.

It's not comfortable, and it's certainly broken, but it's sleep. As when travelling on a plane and having to find a couple of hours here or there between flight meals, I'm slipping in and out with all kinds of fluids leaking from my new face. The nurses come in to take my blood pressure from time to time, which leaves me awake in the dead of night with nothing to think about except the past I'm finally leaving behind.

I can't believe it came to this. After all those years of trying my best to be the perfect wife, Jason eventually pushed me over the edge. It was time to leave, so that's exactly what I did. It was hardly the easiest decision I ever made, and I'm going to be hurting for a long time after this (physically, too, if tonight is anything to go by), but it's for the best.

Now, at long last, I'm free.

Morning comes, although it feels like it's been three days. The sun rose a long time ago, and there's some messing around with paperwork before I'm able to sign out and be on my merry way. The problem is, I haven't heard a thing from Lily. Not so much as a read receipt on my text messages, and my calls aren't going through.

I'm starting to panic. The clinic car park is somewhat vacant, most of the cars simply taking up the spots reserved for staff. There's a bite in the early morning wind, but it's refreshing with all this gauze strapped to my face. That's about as positive as I can get right now, standing here like an idiot and constantly checking my phone.

This isn't like her at all. She's usually so dependable. The Lily I grew up with would have been here a couple of hours early, entertaining herself in the car by singing along to her favourite rock ballads. It makes me wonder if I'm just being blind, so I take a tour of the car park, find nothing, then stand by the doors again and let out a little sigh.

'Something wrong?'

The voice comes from behind me. I would have jumped if I had the energy, but I just turn exhaustedly while rubbing my eyes, careful not to knock the cast on my nose. When I see him standing there, my heart gives off a little, schoolgirl-like flutter that makes my face feel hot. Or *hotter*, I guess I should say.

Cillian looks just as good this time of the morning as he did when I saw him yesterday. Tall and strapping, perfect boy-band-like hair, and a suit that fits him so snugly that I have an easy time imagining what everything looks like under there... and I like what I see.

'No,' I stutter. 'Yes, I mean. My friend is supposed to be here by now.'

'Oh. Do you need a lift somewhere?'

'Maybe. Except I wouldn't know where to go.'

'Where do you live?'

'Bristol.'

Cillian blows out an exaggerated breath. 'That's hours away.'

'Hence, my panic.'

'Would you mind if I waited with you? Call it old-fashioned chivalry.'

My eyes sweep the car park once more. There's nothing good to come from being stranded in such a quiet little town so far from home, but at least I'm in good company. Cillian isn't *just* a doctor – he's a tall, handsome one who already makes me feel safe.

We talk for over an hour, sitting on the bench that overlooks a small garden. I keep checking my phone and glancing around at the car park, only half invested in the conversation, but I do get to learn a lot about him. It sounds like he's of money, which should come as no surprise for a plastic surgeon, and to be completely honest, he comes across as slightly lonely. Not in a creepy way, but in a way that makes me feel a little sorry for him. It's almost endearing.

It's starting to look like Lily isn't going to make it. My messages aren't even being delivered, which raises some alarms, but right now, I need to figure out what I'm going to do. Trying to hide my disappointment, I look around one more time and then put my phone away.

'I'd better find somewhere to stay,' I say. 'Until I can reach my cousin, at least.'

That's when Cillian pulls a face. It's half-wince, half-something else.

'What?' I ask, dread dawning on me.

'You'll be hard-pressed to find somewhere in this town.'

'You're kidding.'

'Nope. I can drive you to the neighbouring town, but you'd be lucky to get a room at short notice. A lot of scenery around here – people come up here for hiking trips, retreats, proposing to their girlfriends. That sort of thing.'

Irritated, I move to scratch my itching chin and then realise I can't. My head is swathed in all this ridiculous padding, which suddenly makes me conscious of how dumb I look in front of the plastic surgeon. 'What would you suggest?'

Cillian exhales. 'It's a shame you can't wait a day, or I could finish off some work and then drive you all the way home. Although I confess, even that would be...'

As he trails off, I start to see some cogs turning behind his eyes. A plan is forming, and I'm already starting to figure it out. At least, I think I am – when he puts it forward to me, I'm a little blown away. Stunned beyond belief, really.

'I'm actually on holiday for the next two weeks,' he says. 'Well, sort of. I'll be staying at home and catching up on some work, research, that kind of thing. This may be extremely forward, but I have plenty of room in my house. You're more than welcome to stay.'

'Oh, no. I couldn't—'

'I understand that, but you're somewhat lacking in options.'

A nervous laugh escapes me. 'That's true.'

'I don't mind taking care of you either. You'll have plenty of bed rest and a professional surgeon under the same roof. I'll give you all the space you need, of course, then I can drive you back home when all my work is done.'

Accepting such an offer would be stupid and dangerous... but I don't really have a choice. It's either this, or stay on the streets in the middle of three invasive surgery recoveries. Going home with this stranger might not be the best option if he turns out to be some psychopath, but how often did men with medical degrees turn out to be creeps?

'Fine,' I say hesitantly. 'If you're sure, I would really appreciate it.'

Cillian smiles that killer smile, then stands and lifts my bag. 'You're in good hands.'

I hope he's right.

Chapter 2
Daisy, Now

THE HOUSE IS AN ABSOLUTE KNOCKOUT. That shouldn't really come as a surprise, but if you saw the place, you'd think it belonged to a lottery winner rather than a surgeon. It's a grand house that looks like it only has one floor, and then another appears behind the slanted roof as you make your way around the drive. My mouth is gaped open the whole time, astonished by the sleek exterior, one wall made entirely of glass, a fancy outdoor pool that looks like it's never been used, and a perfect display of flowers that's so much for one man that it's obvious he has a gardener.

'This place is incredible,' I say in a breath.

Cillian smiles and opens the door, then kicks his heels against the mat. I follow him inside as he gives me the grand tour. It's embarrassing to sound so easily pleased – like a celebrity's fangirl buckling at the knees – but the interior is even more impressive. There are oak beams everywhere, marble surfaces, crystal chandeliers... the works. I know very little (exactly nothing) about housing, but there's no way in hell this house cost less than a cool million.

We walk to the end of a long, spacious hall and up a set of stairs that looks like the *Titanic*'s Grand Staircase. Cillian shows me from room to room. They all look the same, mostly converted into a gym, a small theatre, and a room with nothing in it except a full-size snooker table. At the end of the hall, where a very small window lets in only a slither of light, he opens a door and reveals a gorgeous guest bedroom that's so bright and airy I couldn't possibly imagine feeling anything other than on top of the world.

'This is where you'll be staying,' Cillian says, waving me in. 'You need as much bed rest as possible. The team probably already told you, but you'll need to sleep sitting more or less upright for some time. Are you a side sleeper?'

I nod.

'Not any more. Back only.' His smile softens.

'It's not going to be easy, I promise you that, but you're in very good hands. I'll give you as much space as possible, only stepping in to offer you things here or there. Food and drink will all be taken care of, so just enjoy the TV and bookcase. You'll make your way through a few tomes if you're not too sleepy.'

My gaze drifts to the nearby bookcase, stuffed with Martina Cole, Daniel Hurst, and Colleen Hoover. Exactly my cup of tea, but the mere mention of sleep already tugs at my eyelids. I try not to yawn for fear of looking rude, but it escapes my mouth anyway.

'You need to rest,' Cillian says. 'Make yourself comfortable. If you need anything at all, just make your way downstairs and knock on the first door on the left.'

'What's that room?' I ask out of curiosity.

'The study.'

'Do you spend a lot of time there?'

'My entire life is either in the clinic, the study, or the bed.'

A strange silence grows between us then. It might have something to do with my awkwardness as I begin to imagine Cillian's bed. This is hardly a love story for the ages, but only a madwoman would not find this man insanely attractive. Perhaps he's picked up on my lust, too – his stare lowers to my breasts, lingers for a second, and then he heads for the door.

'The circumstances are strange, but I want you to know you're safe. Please get comfortable, and remember, if you need anything—'

'First door on the left.'

We exchange another long smile, and then he disappears and closes the door behind him. Finally alone, feeling all clogged up and frustrated, I throw myself on to the uniquely comfortable bed and stare up at the rich, beamed ceiling with butterflies in my stomach.

It feels too good to be true.

Usually, that means it is.

DON'T ASK ME HOW, but I somehow managed to get some sleep. At least for a little while – the cast is majorly restricting my breathing, and there's a little discomfort in being all alone in this enormous house with a stranger. A kind, beautiful stranger, but a stranger nonetheless.

A quick glance at the alarm clock tells me it's a

little after two. My eyes are dry and tight, breathing still a struggle. Cillian left a box of tissues on the bedside table for my runny nose, but it's almost empty already. That's how bad it is. And don't even get me started on the irritation of the chin implant and liposuction. Still, in trying to see the positives, I'm at least grateful that I'm female and don't need to shave my neck. I couldn't imagine that.

I watch the clock for over an hour before deciding enough is enough. There's no way I'm getting back to sleep after taking what was essentially an extended nap. The discomfort is too great, bordering on pain, and I can't stop thinking about Lily. What on earth happened to her? How could she just abandon me here, stuck in the middle of nowhere after some pretty aggressive surgery? It's really not like her at all – I hope she's okay.

But there's something else niggling at me. Something that's been on my mind ever since the sky outside started turning dark. Cillian comes across as such a good person, and he's been checking on me every couple of hours all day. Why, then, has he not come to say goodnight? I wonder if I've said something to upset him, which is unlikely, then wonder if maybe something might have happened to him – a trip down the stairs or locked himself in a room. Even less likely, but somewhat plausible when desperate for an explanation.

It gets to four in the morning before I start thinking about just staying up all night. Like Cillian said, there are so many books, and there's a TV on the wall that probably wouldn't wake up my host even if I put it on full blast. There's a soft wind brushing against the window, which would make it nice and cosy if I decided to read, but to be honest, I'm just too tired. Too weak.

Too distracted.

I even thought about just running Netflix off my phone, but I seem to have lost that somewhere over the past few hours. I'd be up and looking for it, but apparently, I'm not allowed to bend over. Something to do with blood pressure to my head or something.

Anyway, I'm getting thirsty, and I've run out of water. If there was ever a time to take a wander around the house, then this is it. And just to be clear, I'm not a snooper in any way, shape, or form, but I need to top up my glass and wouldn't altogether mind bumping into Cillian, even if just to see another human being for the first time in hours.

Sure, the loneliness is getting to me, or perhaps I'm just feeling sorry for myself.

Either way, it's time to get up and explore.

MY KNEES ARE stiff as I slip out of the bed, my heels cracking under my weight. I'm only little – five and a half feet tall and what they call 'yoga thin' – but I'm not used to standing any more. It's amazing what can happen over the course of a day, even with toilet breaks.

The first thing I do is have a quick look for my phone. And I mean *quick*. Like I mentioned, I'm not allowed to lean forward, and this would probably require a more thorough search. I imagine it's slipped off the top of my backpack, possibly into the depths of the open bag itself. It's not really needed right now, but it's nice to know where it is.

Giving up somewhat hastily, I run to the bathroom and do my business, then stand in the long, dark hallway. There's a dim light at the end, coming up the stairs, and I head in that direction on my tiptoes, just in case Cillian is sleeping. The stairs creak as I make my descent, but that's unavoidable. Downstairs, the doors are all closed –

study included – so I make my way around the enormous house in awe once again.

It might just be my worn-out brain, but alarm bells are ringing. I don't care how good a surgeon you are, there's no way you can afford all of this on one man's salary. To give Cillian a little credit, he does come across as really sweet and sincere, so I'll give him the benefit of the doubt and assume that maybe he inherited some money. In films, they talk about medical students living off their parents' riches.

This could be the case, couldn't it?

I wander farther, becoming more and more convinced that my generous host is in bed and had simply left this light on to warn off potential intruders. Not that anyone is even around to break in here. There's nobody around for miles – we're surrounded by a range of the greenest fields, which are now just black canvasses in the dead of night.

When I find the long glass wall in the living room, I stand there and watch the moonlight dance off the tiny ripples of the outside pool. It's so beautiful to watch, but the thought of water sends a chill right through me. I'm at peace for all of a minute, distracted by the beauty of nature's elements, right up until my nose runs again. It's a harsh reminder of my long recovery, but somebody would probably always be around to say I did this to myself.

Yeah, as if I had a choice.

'Having trouble sleeping?'

Cillian's voice makes me jump out of my skin. I scream, spot his reflection in the glass, then awkwardly laugh while feeling silly. As I turn to look at him, he brightens the dimmer bulb and fills the doorway. God, even in shorts and a T-shirt, he looks so good.

'Sorry,' he says with a smile. 'That's twice I've made you startle.'

'It's okay. It's just unfamiliar territory, you know?'

'I get it. Do you need something?'

'Actually, I wouldn't mind a glass of water.'

'Where's your glass?'

My hand rises to gently slap my own forehead. 'Forgot it. Duh.'

Cillian laughs and waves me in his direction, beckoning me to follow him all the way to the kitchen. This is even more impressive. It's so big you could run laps around the massive marble island. There's a huge oven that's even bigger than my entire kitchen and a range of see-through pantry doors that are fully stocked. Cillian takes a glass from one of them and fills it from the refrigerator's filter system. He hands it to me, and I thank him.

'Have you seen my phone anywhere?' I ask after a small sip.

'Can't say that I have. Aren't you supposed to be resting though?'

'Couldn't sleep.'

'You should probably try.'

'I did.'

'Then try harder.'

An uncomfortable chuckle escapes me, but Cillian's smile doesn't budge. He just watches me as if expecting more – like we're in an interview and he's waiting for a more elaborate reaction. I'm suddenly aware of just how easy it would be for him to do something to me, which sends a bolt of ice right through me. All it took was a few short seconds to go from fully comfortable to extremely wary. It's not even the look that's done it to me. There's something else, but it's hard to put my finger on exactly.

'You're right,' I tell him. 'I'm going to give it another shot. Thanks for the water.'

Cillian's smile broadens. 'My pleasure. Good-night, Daisy.'

On my way back up the stairs, I keep looking over my shoulder to see if he's following. He's not, which makes me feel like I'm just being a little paranoid. To bare my soul, I'm feeling at my most vulnerable after what happened with my ex, and the surgery is taking its toll on me. What I really need is a good night's sleep, so I crawl into bed and try again.

It only takes a minute to realise why I was so uncomfortable downstairs. It wasn't Cillian's smile at all, and nor was it his words. It was something else that drew a dark cloud over my head, the image of that memory leaping out at me from nowhere as if to ring those alarm bells all over again.

No, it wasn't the smile at all but the thought of every window in the house.

And the bars on every one of them.

Chapter 3
Daisy, Then

LIFE WAS SO DIFFERENT, even as little as a year ago.

I was ugly, of course. That's what Jason kept telling me. Wasn't he supposed to love me regardless of anything? That's what Lily kept saying – that a real man will love you no matter how you look. I didn't necessarily subscribe to that, but he definitely fancied me to begin with. I had no idea what changed, but he'd stopped looking at me with affection and lust. Now, he only looked at me with contempt.

On this particular day, he was out at work. Jason was very old-fashioned, expecting a meal on the table in a clean house after a long day of fixing pipes and unclogging drains. Most women would run a mile at that sort of set-up, but it worked for me. I had some savings (which I'd later spend on surgeries), and we didn't need much. Just a roof over our heads, enough food to keep my man slightly overweight, and a TV licence to entertain us on those evenings we weren't pissing away his earnings at the local pub. It was a simple life, and that was all I'd ever wanted, so what was there to complain about, really?

Well... there was the way he treated me.

It's one thing to be told you're ugly, but another thing entirely to be constantly reminded how much you disgust someone. It was becoming something of a ritual for Jason, and it'd started after his mother died. I tried to let it go at first, deciding he was so angry at the world that he'd needed someone to take it out on. I thought he loved me, so I shrugged it off, but somewhere over time, it started to grate on me. Gone were the days of flowers, soft kisses, and constant compliments. Now, I was standing at the sink and washing up the pans I'd just used to make dinner, watching the clock and dreading his return from work.

But to be honest... I wasn't happy. I'd always wanted surgery, but each time he made a comment, I just thought more and more about what I'd have done. My nose was obvious – I'd been bullied about that all the way through school – but my weak chin and the fat surrounding it was starting to play on my mind. Every time I looked in the mirror, I saw a glimmer of what Jason must have seen.

And it made me feel disgusting.

On top of feeling like the ugly duckling, I also felt ashamed. Not just for my appearance but for letting the man I loved walk all over me. While I scrubbed away at a stubborn sauce stain inside the big saucepan, I found myself grinding my teeth and wondering if I really loved him any more. That fun, kind, sensitive man I'd fallen for hadn't made an appearance in months. In his place was a nasty, spiteful piece of work who just *loved* to put me down.

I'd had enough... almost.

The van pulled up outside, the low grumble shaking through our tiny house. My heartbeat started speeding, my head going light as I glanced at the clock one last time. I peered around the room to make sure everything was just how he liked it, propped the washed pan on to the rack, then untied my apron and moved the hot food out of the oven and on to the table.

I was just in time to hear the front door open. Steeling myself for yet another round of abuse, I stood up straight and prepared to take whatever this man threw at me. The only thing that got me through the anxiety of waiting for this to happen was knowing that somewhere deep inside me was a strong woman in charge of her own fate.

And crunch time was coming.

I could feel it.

PICTURE A STEREOTYPICAL TRADESMAN who's big without working out, has the sort of eyes that look nice in the right light but mean in the wrong one, and throw in a menacing presence that's easily mistaken for being an attractive manly feature.

That was Jason.

It'd been easy to fall in love with him, especially after buying all my drinks and whispering sweet nothings into my ear. We'd gone home together from the bar that night and slept together right away, quickly entering into a relationship that outlived the love between us. It'd been seven years, and my patience was starting to wear thin.

As was my courage to stand up to him.

Jason stomped through the house as he kicked off his shoes like a teenager, storming right into the kitchen. It was hard not to see that he was looking at the dinner table before even laying an eye on me. That told me everything I needed to know about his priorities.

'How was work?' I asked nervously, basically dying for normal conversation.

'Ugh,' he grunted, pulling out a chair and tucking into the curry I'd prepared.

'Do you want a beer with your food?'

'I always have a beer with food. You should know that by now.'

Trying not to roll my eyes, I took a bottle from the fridge, removed the cap, and put it beside him. This was always the hardest part of the day: sitting beside an ungrateful pig of a man who hated me and trying to encourage myself to eat. I somehow managed just like I did every other day, but I left a portion aside just because it was hard to stomach.

In no time at all, Jason finished his meal, burped, downed the beer, then turned his stare on me while chomping whatever remains lingered in his mouth. It was the look that always forced me to look away – the look that frightened the hell out of me.

'What have you done today? Nothing as usual?'

'Not exactly. The house is clean, and you just ate the food I cooked.'

'It's curry, Daisy. It doesn't exactly take much effort.'

Why don't you do it then? I thought.

'What else?' Jason shoved his plate away and sat back, clasping his hands over his paunch. 'Come on, you can't tell me all you did was run the hoover around and throw some ingredients into the pan?'

'That's... exactly what I did.' Frailty enters my croaking voice, but I somehow manage to hide it. *Just.* 'Also, I cut the grass, changed the bedding, then put my feet up for a few minutes. Sometimes it gets tiring looking after a house all by myself.'

Jason grunted again. 'You think that's tough, try doing a whole day's work.'

'Well, I used to. Before giving it up.'

'Maybe you should get your job back, then, if it bothers you that much.'

'They won't take me back.'

'Then get a new one. Try prostitution or some-thing. Then again, maybe not – given how you look, you'd be the one having to pay the men.'

Although his full-belly laugh made it clear how funny he found that, it *really* hurt. Like I said before, this wasn't the first time he'd made a reference to how ugly I was, and it was getting tiresome to hear. Not just annoying but *exhausting*. There's only so many times a woman can hear things like that before real depression sets in.

By the time the laughter stopped, I was ready to cry. Jason studied me then, his stare creeping over me like an army of ants. My head tucked down, I avoided his gaze so as not to antagonise him. But that only lasted until he said my name.

'Daisy...'

'What?'

'Get me another beer.'

I knew where this was going. My hands shook in my lap. Bad news was about to come his way, which meant it would then come back on me. I swallowed a lump and shook my head, then tried opening my dry mouth to tell him.

'That's the last one. I didn't get a chance to—'

In the blink of an eye, Jason shot to his feet. I didn't see him hurl the bottle, but I jumped a mile when it exploded into shards of glass as it hit the wall. The stink of beer puffed into the air immediately, but it was drowned out by Jason's hot breath as he leaned over me.

'You had time to put your feet up, but you couldn't be bothered to go shopping!' he screamed. 'How bloody hard is it to run to the shop and pick up a few things for the man who pays your bills? For crying out loud!'

It took everything I had not to sob in the silence that followed. Jason had never hit me, but I lived in constant fear that he someday would. I'd seen violent men before, and this was always how it started. Somehow, my husband had become a ticking time bomb.

After a torturous eternity, he finally huffed and left the room. Seconds later, the front door slammed, and I would have a few hours to myself while he spent the evening at the pub. Most women would hate this, but I kind of enjoyed the fact he'd be out of my hair for a spell. It gave me time to reflect on the relationship – on my life – and it didn't take very long at all to realise that the time had finally come. It was time for me to pack up and leave.

If I could only bring myself to do it.

It was midnight when he clumsily rolled into bed. The stench of alcohol alone was enough to wake me up, but I hadn't been sleeping anyway. My head was buzzing with the fear and excitement of starting a new life. Somewhere fresh. Somewhere far away from him.

Although the scars would remain forever.

They weren't physical scars, but enough comments had been made to poison the rest of my life. My confidence was at an all-time low, my opinion of myself the lowest it'd ever been. How was I supposed to go on living while looking the way I looked? How was I ever expected to look in the mirror without feeling completely worthless?

It was this alarming thought that inspired me to move. I waited, of course, giving it a sleepless couple of hours to ensure Jason was fully wiped out, the alcohol knocking him into his usual coma. Then, holding my breath as I went, I slowly slipped out of bed and opened the drawers underneath. My clothes were in neat piles (nothing new there), which made it easier to just grab a handful and leave the bedroom quietly. I didn't bother closing the door behind me – the last thing I wanted was for the click to wake him up.

Finally out of the bedroom, I was free to walk

around without worrying too much about being quiet. Our house was cheap, but the walls were thick. I made quick work of pulling out the suitcase from under the stairs and stuffing it with the clothes I'd grabbed. I kept stopping to think about which toiletries to pack, but really, it was probably an excuse to just talk myself out of it. Isn't it funny how the mind works?

A few minutes later, that was it. My bag was packed, a taxi was on its way, and I was standing outside waiting for it while praying Jason wouldn't wake up to my absence. What would even happen then? How would I explain myself? Would he finally break and hit me?

This was the wildness that'd made me uncomfortable in the first place.

The taxi came in minutes. I shoved the suitcase on to the back seat beside me just to save time, then sat quietly as the drive took me away from my old life. My heart was pounding the whole time, and I couldn't believe this was finally happening. In such a short space of time, Jason had gone from being my biggest problem to just a terrible memory.

And I didn't feel the slightest bit bad about it.

Chapter 4
Daisy, Now

ON THE SURFACE, it's easy to say Cillian is a good host.

Let's face it, three solid meals per day plus snacks and frequent check-ups is hardly a bad deal. Especially when it's free. Yet I still can't stop thinking about the bars on those windows. They were only on the downstairs ones, but it still struck me as strange. The decor in this incredible house is a feast for the eyes, everything new and shiny and expensive... so then, why the eyesore? What possible reason could he have for locking down the house with hideous iron when everything else looks so magnificent?

That's why I asked him.

'They were here when I moved in,' he said. 'I just never got around to removing them.'

I've been thinking about that non-stop ever since. If I wanted to believe it – really *wanted* to – there was a chance of persuading myself that he was telling the truth. To be fair, there are still a couple of things in the house that look unfinished: the banister still needs sanding, and there's a large patch of grass outside that is yet to grow out of its turf. It's altogether possible that the bars still need removing. The only thing that tells me otherwise is that they're shiny.

They look new.

I'm not going to let it get to me. There's enough going on with my face being in so much pain. My neck is stiff and sore from having to sleep elevated, the pillows not quite doing the best job of supporting me. I've just had my third night in this house, and Cillian came in with a wonderful breakfast for me. There was toast, cereal, orange juice, and coffee (decaf, as I'm unfortunately not allowed caffeine for another four days – booooooo). It went down a treat, but ever since he said he was going to shower, I've had my heart set on exploiting that opportunity.

The second I hear the shower run, I roll out of

bed, then tiptoe carefully out of the room and down the hall. There's movement under the running water, a clear sign I'm free to go and roam the house for just a few minutes. I already know where I want to go, and I slide into his office without so much as having to turn the doorknob.

It's exactly what you can expect from a rich plastic surgeon. Oak everywhere, leather-bound books on the vast shelves along the enormous walls, and a desk big enough to support both Jack *and* Rose in the North Atlantic Ocean.

'Everything is so perfect,' I mumble under my breath, heading straight for his computer.

There's no security on the computer, which makes my task even easier. You'd think I would go searching through his personal files, but all I really need to know is how long I must stay here. Cillian says it's at least two weeks and maybe even longer, but a quick Google search says one week should be enough. The cast could then be removed from my nose, and I'll be fit to start light exercise, such as walking. I could take care of myself from that point on.

As long as he lets me.

I shake my head at the thought. He hasn't said or done anything to suggest that he'll keep me locked up in this house, but the mind wanders. All I want is some reassurance that I'm safe here – that the bars on the windows are just remnants of the house's previous owner. It's all looking good until I see the website history and find—

'What are you doing in here?'

I shoot upright at the sound of his voice. Panic flutters through me. Heat rises to my cheeks. I didn't hear the water stop – how could I? The walls are so damn thick that I couldn't even hear Cillian coming down the stairs. Now, he's standing there wearing only jeans, a towel hanging around his sculpted shoulders. And under his wet hair and serious eyebrows?

An angry, accusatory scowl.

To TELL THE TRUTH, I don't think I've done anything *that* wrong. Sure, I was snooping around in a room I had no business being in, but is it really the end of the world? Judging by the look on Cillian's face – his dark eyes somehow turning even darker as his gaze levels on me – I've done something so wrong it could be considered sinister.

'Cillian' is all I can get out.

It feels like the longest minute of my life. All he does is stand there, staring right through me as if I'm not there. As if he's deep in thought and reliving the worst memory of his life. A cold shiver shoots through me like lightning, and all of a sudden, I feel hopelessly vulnerable in my pyjamas. It takes a minute to realise why that is: I'm not wearing shoes.

Which would make it hard to run.

After an agonisingly long breath, Cillian stalks across the room and around the desk. I step to one side as he leans over and studies the computer, his brow furrowed. He looks like a scientist studying a specimen with such fierce intensity that the whole room has gone cold.

'What were you looking at on here?' he asks. No – *demands*.

'Nothing,' I blurt out nervously. 'I just wanted to read about my recovery.'

'You didn't think to just ask?'

It's hard to think of better wording than 'I wanted a second opinion', so I simply shrug and bite my lower lip. I regret that immediately, of course, as my chin makes a movement inside my compression garment that scratches my sensitive neck. It stings.

Cillian taps away at the keyboard, quickly shutting down Windows before turning off the monitor. Resting on his knuckles that are planted on his desk, he stares at the blank screen with that dazed look again. Anyone would think his entire world just ended. It makes me think he has something to hide. Something other than what I saw in his history, that is.

Finally, he huffs and turns to stare at me again, setting his jaw.

'What did you find?' he asks.

'Nothing, really. It just says I could be gone in under a week.'

'Two weeks,' he corrects.

'But the website says—'

'Who cares what the website says?'

'I do. Since my phone went missing, and I can't google things—'

'Do we have some kind of trust issue here?' he snaps.

An awkward silence follows, during which it feels like there's nothing I can say or do to excuse myself. Then, causing me to instinctively step back, he reaches out to feed his fingertips under my garment. It's not enough to strangle me, but it's enough to make me wish I was somewhere else. Literally anywhere else. Even hell would do.

'How tight is it?' he asks, glossing over his previous question.

'It's a little restrictive.'

'That's for the best. It should improve your results.'

'If you're sure.'

Cillian sighs. It's obvious he doesn't like being questioned, but what's a girl to do? I'm locked in a house in the middle of nowhere, my phone is missing, there are bars on the windows, and the only person to share my time with is showing signs of anger.

I feel helpless.

What happens next is completely unexpected. Cillian reaches out for my hand and takes it lightly, but as he leads me out of the room, I feel a slight ferociousness in how hard he tugs. It's like I'm being towed out to the hallway and to the bottom of the stairs. He stops there, cutting me off along with him, and locks his stare on me.

'Let's make something completely clear,' he says, clearly wearing a see-through calmness that really doesn't match the intensity in his eyes. 'When I give you aftercare instructions for your surgeries, they're not suggestions. They're orders. If you stray from those, your results *will* be impacted, and your results won't look how you want them to. Is that something you really want to risk after spending thousands on all these alterations?'

I shake my head, feeling like a schoolgirl being told off. This isn't right. I shouldn't feel like a prisoner here, and I certainly haven't done anything wrong except take an innocent little snoop. Is that really so bad? Does that really warrant the strictness he's talking at me with?

'No' is all that comes out of my quivering lips. 'It's not worth the risk.'

'So then, you'll trust me?'

'Whatever the doctor orders.'

I try to smile with that, but it falls short. Cillian's eyes bore right through me, like he's making a cold, heartless calculation. It makes me question my safety here, but it's hard to say if that's an overreaction. One might argue he's just taking care of his patient. Very firm care, admittedly, but care all the same. That's how it might look on the outside anyway.

Being here is a different thing entirely.

'We have an understanding, then?' he says.

'I'll do as I'm told, yes.'

'That's all I ask.'

Cillian's features soften, and it's like a rain cloud has passed. The sunshine pours through now, everything lighter, happier... better. I should feel warm and safe with that look on his face, but it'll be hard to forget the way he's been speaking to me these past few minutes. I've never felt so bad for doing so little, which is why my eyes sweep towards the door. I return my gaze to him quickly enough that he doesn't notice, and thank God for that.

Because he probably wouldn't react very well.

'Get yourself back to bed,' he says calmly. 'Have some rest.'

'Okay,' I say in submission. 'Sorry for looking around.'

'That's okay. Just don't let it happen again.'

As I walk up the stairs, I can't help thinking I've just got away with something. Like I've survived something I really had no business surviving. The fatigue caused by my surgeries might just be making me sensitive and causing me to overreact, but I feel how I feel despite how it would look on paper. Like they say, trust your gut.

Why, then, am I not doing what my gut says?

Why am I not packing up and running?

———

Look, I know I'm not allowed to lean forward, but that doesn't stop me from taking another thorough search for my phone. I realised just a couple of minutes ago that it might be affecting my view of this whole situation. If I had my phone, I'd have contact with the outside world. If I had that, I wouldn't feel so isolated.

If I wasn't isolated, I wouldn't be so scared.

The pressure shoots through my head and starts to throb. I toss some clothes aside while frantically looking for it. It must be here somewhere, but it doesn't magically appear no matter how many times I look. What the hell happened to it?

Giving up, I lower myself on to the bed and start thinking about Lily. Surely, she must be wondering where I am by now, and God knows what happened to her. She's usually so dependable, and it's really out of character for her to not stay in contact at the very least.

Not that it's the biggest of my concerns. I'm unsettled, my foot tapping against the foot of the bed as I run through my findings in my head. It wasn't just the surgical guidelines that threw me, nor the scolding from Cillian himself, but the *other* thing I saw on his computer...

There was the internet window he'd already opened.

I breezed over it so quickly that I barely had time to digest it at first. Now that I have time to think, feeling less flustered from being caught by Cillian, it's safe to say I have reason to worry. The bars on the windows were left over from the house's previous owner. That's what Cillian told me, and I really did try to believe him. But the page on his computer showed him searching for those bars and a tradesman to install them. So not only did he lie to me, but now I have another question burning a hole in my mind: what does he need them for? The answer is obvious, but I don't want to admit it because it will drive me mad with panic.

Still, the answer is there, right in front of me.

The bars are there for me.

Chapter 5
Daisy, Now

At least mealtimes are pleasant.

Cillian and I don't talk much as we sit in the grand dining room to eat our dinner. There's mellow jazz playing from one of the speakers that are wired into the wall, and the room is dimly lit to hit a relaxed mood. It works, too, as I feel perfectly safe and calm.

Even given the circumstances.

The food is also remarkable. There's a decent-sized steak (I'm guessing twelve ounces) without a fraction of fat. It's served with mashed potatoes and a variety of green vegetables that I quickly pour the peppercorn sauce all over. The smell itself is enough to make even a bloated woman feel starving. My stomach is in hungry knots as the steam rises past my vision.

The only thing making me uncomfortable now is the pain.

The compression garment is so tight that it's starting to hurt my neck. It's sweaty, too, which means I'm not at my most flattering. I pull at the lower part of the fabric just to loosen the grip around my throat, then reach for my fork all over again.

'You can take that off, you know.' Cillian points at my face. 'Briefly.'

'Really?'

'Yes. It won't hurt to slip it off for meals. Just like you do for showers.'

Naturally, I don't hesitate for even a second. I rip off the Velcro so fast it makes a screaming sound, and I dump the garment to the side of my plate for after. The release is immediate, the air touching my skin and the pain alleviating gradually over the course of seconds. I can't help but smile when granted such freedom.

If only I could remove the nose cast.

'How does that feel?' he asks.

'Amazing. And this' – I circle over the plate with my cutlery – 'looks even better.'

'I'm glad you like it.'

We eat in silence for the most part, the flavours exploding on my tongue. This isn't the first time I've eaten well here, and I'm always quick to compliment Cillian. Mostly because it makes him smile, but he's also very humble when it comes to his culinary skills.

'It was prepared for me,' he always says. 'All I did was throw it together.'

It's hard to tell if he's just being a good guy or if he's telling the truth. He's certainly showed himself to be a smart man with many talents, and it wouldn't surprise me in the slightest if cooking turned out to be one of them. Much like surgery, I imagine it requires a good knowledge of procedure, skill, and the ability to know what to do when things go south.

Thankfully, he's good with his hands.

After the main course, Cillian promises a tiramisu will shortly arrive. I've never had it before, and he claims not to have a sweet tooth, so I accept it gracefully. He disappears into the kitchen, demanding I stay and let him take care of our empty plates, then leaves me to let my food go down while enjoying the piano medley in peace.

The problem is it takes too long for him to return.

I keep an eye on the clock, watching five minutes go by, then ten. I'm starting to feel a little awkward, like I should be doing something to help out. I quickly decide that five more minutes would be an appropriate time to make the move, and that time rolls by too quickly.

Putting my garment back on and getting out of the chair, I go for the door Cillian left for, then find myself in a maze of hallways I haven't seen before. Two of them are open with lights beaming through the gaps, so I head towards those carefully while hoping not to bump into Cillian if he's holding a fragile dessert. The last thing I want to do is upset him any further.

There's a clattering sound coming from the farthest room, like china and cutlery jingling together. I head in that direction, but before I can take a couple more steps, something else catches my eye. Something that almost makes my heart stop dead.

In the other open room, sitting on the side, is a familiar object. My breath catches in my throat as I step inside and reach for it. I'm hoping it's not what I think it is – just because of the implication – but when it's physically in my hands, there's no denying it. I've been looking for this so desperately, and now the only explanation is that Cillian stole it from me.

Cillian stole my phone.

IT USUALLY TAKES a lot to freak me out, but I'm feeling pretty damn vulnerable right now. I haven't even been able to move – I simply stare down at the phone in my hands with questions buzzing through my head. Why did he take this? When? Does that mean I'm able to get out of here if I could only contact someone? How would I go about that?

The voice in my head feels real, the questions coming thick and fast. So fast, in fact, that it takes me a while to realise one of them *is* real. Except it's not my voice at all. It's Cillian's, and it's coming from the doorway behind me.

'Did you hear me?' he asks. Then, as I turn and his sight lowers to the phone in my hand, his face instantly transforms from one of simple curiosity to a contorted expression of anger. His mouth opens, words about to form. Then it's as if he forgets them while his darker emotions take over. 'What the hell do you think you're doing in here?'

'I... Why is my phone—?'

'Excuse me, but I'm asking the questions here.' He jerks a finger towards my chest. 'I've told you before that it's rude to wander. Why would you disobey me twice in a row, Daisy? What exactly are you hoping to achieve?'

Look, I hate confrontation at the best of times. It only gets harder when the man standing in front of you is flushing with red-hot rage. I'm so distracted by his temper that it takes me a while to realise the phone is shaking in my hand. This has to be the most terrified I've been ever since... well, ever since Jason.

But I've stood up to Jason before. That's what I have to keep reminding myself. If I could do that to the man I loved – a decidedly bigger man – there's no reason I can't make it through this. I stand up straight, set my jaw, and ask the question.

'Why is my phone in here?'

Cillian freezes. I'm guessing he's not used to being confronted. His lips move once again, stumbling while he searches for answers. Then his shoulders sag, his features soften, and he takes one slow step into the room. I stiffen but stand my ground.

'You weren't supposed to come in here,' he says calmly.

'Don't change the subject. You took my phone. Why?'

'It's... I had to.'

'*Why?*'

'Because you were thinking of leaving.' He takes a breath, pausing at a crucial time – a time that raises a thousand alarms. 'I've invested a lot of time and energy into you, Daisy. I could see you were looking at alternative methods for your surgical aftercare, and I was scared you were going to ruin things for yourself. It would have undone my hard work, which isn't a very kind way to treat your host. Don't you think?'

I can barely believe what I'm hearing. Does he honestly believe it's acceptable to steal someone's phone and then deny all knowledge of it? Combining this with his anger when I looked at the computer, then factoring in the dulling blue in his eyes, I'm starting to question if he's playing with a full deck. The warmth is gone. What remains is ice-cold.

'Cillian, you had no right taking my phone.'

'And you had no right snooping around my house.'

'That's not relevant to the fact—'

'*I will decide what's relevant!*'

The deep booming in his voice makes me gasp. The phone slips from my hands, and I take the step back that I've been wanting. Cillian's neck veins are pulsating, his face growing redder as his eyes alight with fury. Suddenly, the compression mask feels like it's strangling me, and my breath is getting harder to stabilise.

I'm frozen. I don't know what to say or do. Cillian is glaring at me. I try to speak, but my lower lip is quivering too much, and my voice might break at the first attempt. The silence grows in the room, the tension mounting. It's the kind of uncomfortable air that the slightest sudden sound might make me scream.

Then... he bends to pick up the phone.

It's hard, but I have to speak up.

'Give me the phone, Cillian.'

'Not a chance.'

I hold out my hand, words hissing through my teeth. 'Give me the phone.'

'You're in no position to make demands.'

'I want to leave. Please give me back my phone.'

'You're not leaving.'

'It's not like you can stop me.'

'Wrong.'

I close my eyes and take a deep, steadying breath. It lasts for all of a second before I open them just to watch him. I quickly remember the bars on the windows, the explosion of anger when he found me in his office. The rage he displayed only seconds ago. Then it all becomes clear: he's not just unstable...

He's insane.

It's almost impossible to do, but I have to put my foot down and make my intentions clear. My hands still rattling with fear, I straighten up again and tell him as it is. 'Whether you give me back my phone or not, I'm leaving.'

'No, you're not.'

Without hesitation, I go for the door.

Cillian steps in my way. 'You're going nowhere. Nobody will help you.'

'I'll walk into town if I have to.'

'You'd have to get out of the house first.'

My heart is racing so fast it's about to burst from my chest. 'Let me go, Cillian.'

'No chance.'

'I want to leave. Please stand aside.'

'What about your recovery?'

'I'll figure it out.'

'Not without me, you won't.'

'Well, that's not your decision to make.'

That's all I can say or do to talk him down. It's clear he won't listen, which leaves me with no choice but to step out of my comfort zone. Doing all I can to hide my fear, I remind myself of all I've been through. Then, with adrenaline coursing through me like fire, I fix my gaze on the door, take a quick breath, then try to run.

That's when all hell breaks loose.

I FEEL the tug at my hair before anything else. It's sharp and forceful, like clumps are being torn out. I lose my balance and stumble, reaching for anything to grab on to as a scream rips through my throat. The pain is excruciating, the shock paralysing.

'Please stop,' I try to say, but my voice is breezy and pathetic. It comes out in a whimper, and trying again doesn't change anything. All I can do is scream and cry, digging my heels into the floor as Cillian drags me up the stairs.

'Stop fighting it!' he barks, still pulling at my hair.

The steps tug at my shorts as I'm dragged, the carpet burning the skin on my legs. I'm trying to stand upright, panic bolting through me while I also try to push him away. My scalp is on fire, but before I know it, we're back upstairs. The distance between us and my bedroom is closing. For a moment, I think it's not so bad – that all he'll do is toss me inside, and then I can maybe make a run for it when he's not looking.

But then that hope is torn from me.

By the time Cillian lets go of my hair, I'm back in the bedroom. I reach up to massage my scalp, fighting off tears and recovering from my near fall. By then, the door slams shut. The room shakes. A fearful void opens in my heart. Not just from his aggressive outburst and not even from how hard he threw me into this room.

But at the sound of the key turning in the lock.

And the grim realisation that I'm trapped.

Chapter 6
Jason, Now

IT's bloody shocking that she thinks she can get away from me.

Maybe I'm no cop, no private investigator or whatever, but I've got a brain. I've also got a phone, the number to our local taxi office, and my own car. After learning that Daisy sneaked into a cab in the middle of the night, it was just a matter of calling them and explaining her mental health issues. She doesn't really have any – except for the question of that one outburst, maybe – but they don't need to know that. As long as I was convincing when telling the story, which I was, they would hand over the details about where they took her...

Which they did.

Now, I'm sitting in a café on the outskirts of Whereverthefuck, newspaper folded on to the table and a steaming latte burning a scent into the air around me. The phone in my hand has a history of text messages between Daisy and the man she's supposed to love, but all I'm seeing in these words is a weak, placating woman with no brains, no courage, or both.

She didn't come across that way at the time. She always seemed so content, getting worked up about the outbursts from time to time before shrinking into the background. That has been her personality since the day I met her. She is, in a word, meek.

I've got to admit, though, what she did was a very ballsy move. I'd be surprised if I didn't lift up her skirt to find an impressive set of testicles. Never in a million years would I have thought she'd do that, leaping into a taxi and saying goodbye forever.

Except it's not goodbye, is it?

Because I'm on to her.

This café is exactly where the taxi left her. The woman at the counter said they exchanged a few words, and Daisy is on her way to a small town just a few hours north. I'll get there soon enough, just as soon as I've filled up on caffeine and good food. Whatever her reasons for heading specifically in this direction, she hasn't got away from me. Not even close.

She's going to pay for what she did.

Chapter 7
Daisy, Then

It was my first night miles from home, and I didn't even have Jason for comfort. Usually, he would be there to hold my hand and tell me everything was going to be okay. That's how he was with me to begin with, at least. Before he became nasty.

It had only been a day, and I was already starting to miss him. It was true that he scared the living hell out of me, but there was a sort of familiarity that came with having him around. I tried to tell myself it was just cowardice worming its way into my subconscious, trying to convince me that I should head back and start grovelling.

But that wasn't going to happen.

I was stronger than Jason had ever made me feel. I'd come this far, hadn't I? Nobody had helped me pack my bags, nobody had lined up to say goodbye or lent me money for that taxi. I checked into the hotel with my own money, standing on my own two feet to start over. It felt good to be independent, but somewhere deep inside me was this cavernous gap... and it was filled with anxiety and dread.

Throughout the night, I kept falling asleep and dreaming very vividly that he had come for me. It felt so real when he grabbed my throat that I kept waking up to check my neck in the mirror. There was no bruise, of course, but it was disturbing enough to keep me unsettled. While I was up, I opened the curtain and sat by the window, watching the long, empty road and expecting Jason to pull up any minute now. As I stared, half-asleep and dry-eyed, a light rain started tapping against the glass. Rain had always settled me, and sleep wasn't going to happen anytime soon, so I dragged a small armchair across the room and sat to watch it.

This was where the real dark thoughts started to creep in. While I watched the rain get heavier and pat against the dimly lit street, I started drifting into a memory of when Jason had first yelled at me. Everything had been perfect until that moment – we'd been together for almost a year without so much as a slight disagreement – but I'd misplaced his dead father's watch when cleaning the house. Jason's voice had understandably got louder and more desperate as we searched the house together, and although he didn't hit me, he did raise his hand. Our eyes had met, the pair of us fully understanding how close he'd just come to striking his own girlfriend. Jason then lowered his hand and continued searching.

We never did find the watch.

Maybe that's why he started hating me.

It felt like such a long time ago. I always loved that man, but our romance had come to an end long before I packed my bags. If you think about it, nothing was really missing. It was just an adjustment period – that was what I told myself – and I would soon adapt to being single again after all those years. For now, I just had to get some sleep and then move on to the next hotel first thing in the morning, slowly inching farther and farther away from my home.

In a way, it was kind of exciting.

Even if it did make me cry.

THE NEXT MORNING, I was running on about three hours of broken sleep. I got all the way to nine o'clock before realising it just wasn't going to happen, so I did everything I could to perk myself up. So began a sort of healing process: a shower, cooked breakfast in the hotel's restaurant, and a short walk around the local area to see what it had to offer. I made it two-thirds through that plan before the lady at reception stopped me.

'Did he find you, Mrs. Campbell?'

My heart stopped as I turned to face her. My stony gaze fixed on the young receptionist. She couldn't have been older than twenty, her chestnut hair pulled taut into a ponytail. She gave a thin, courteous smile as she awaited a response. I just didn't know what to say.

'Did who find me?'

'The man who was looking for you.' She paused long enough to figure out that I had no idea who she was talking about, then leaned slightly over the desk. 'Around six o'clock this morning, someone came to the desk looking for you. At least, I *think* it was you. The woman he described matched you perfectly, and he did give your first name.'

Terror seized me, words struggling to come. 'He... How...?'

But the receptionist nodded understanding. 'Don't worry, we're not actually allowed to share information with strangers. No matter how much he begged, I was pretty firm in telling him I wasn't going to search the database.'

'I really appreciate that. Is he still here?'

'Nope. He tried finding a loophole, showing me a photo of you and asking if I'd at least seen you enter the building. I quickly got the sense that he had some kind of problem with you, so I just shook my head and apologised.'

'Then what happened?'

'He just thanked me and walked away.'

I sagged with relief. So, he had come for me after all. It didn't surprise me in the slightest, but hearing the story did make me shudder. How had he even got this far? Was I that obvious? As far as I knew, nobody had any access to my banking history, so it wasn't like the hotel would have showed up on my statement. Especially not so soon.

Before I left, the receptionist assured me that the man was long gone. Apparently, he'd talked about moving on to the next town (which encouraged me to head in the other direction) and that I was free to explore the local area before setting off. The hotel room had been feeling more like a prison cell, so I was determined to see my morning plan through before deciding where to go. Obviously, my options were now more limited.

I thanked the receptionist one more time, appreciating the feeling of sisterhood. Us women had to stick together – there were plenty of creeps out there, and for all she knew, a stalker had just turned up looking for me. That was true in a sense, but I thought of him more like a hunter than a stalker. He knew who he was looking for, and he was desperate to get me.

At least the town was beautiful. It was constructed mostly of stone, reminding me of Bath. Last night's rain still lingered, and I took in deep breaths of its remaining scent. It settled me a little as I walked around the local market, treating myself to two small bags of fudge, some hot chocolate, and a new jacket. It helped me appreciate the smaller things in life.

But it didn't stop me from seeing his face everywhere.

I knew it wasn't real. Jason was now a thing of the past, no matter where he was, but I saw his eyes on the face of a tradesman, his sneer in the wondrous expression of a baby, and his rain-matted hair over an old man's forehead. It truly felt like I couldn't get away from him – like he was following me, stalking me, letting me know there was no way to ever break free.

There wasn't a sane woman in the world who could live with that.

For the rest of the morning, I tried my hardest to put it out of my mind. The closest I got to moving on was to sit in a pub and snack on a bowl of French fries while mapping out the rest of my journey. I traced my finger along the map, trying to figure out where he might have gone next. The obvious answer would be a small village south-east of here, but only because it led to a bigger city. Plenty of job opportunities and places to live. Somewhere to start a new life. That might not be how *he* would see it, but he'd probably thought I did.

Which was exactly why I was going in a different direction.

Satisfied, I finished my fries and downed the Diet Coke, packed up my things, then decided to take one last stroll around the bustling street. It was extremely busy for such a small place, but I didn't mind one bit – it helped me blend in. Helped me hide... like a coward.

I shrugged off that feeling as best I could, but it all collapsed when I saw him.

It only happened for a second. A break in the crowd let me see his face. Angry, tall, and staring at me like he wanted revenge for what I did to him. It took my breath away as if I'd fallen in icy water, but by the time I could confirm what I saw, the crowd merged back together and obstructed my view.

I was alone then, stranded in the market with an eerie chill running up and down my spine. Was he here or not? Was he watching me, or had he moved on to locate me already? Whatever the case, one thing became immediately clear.

It was time to leave.

———

I HANDED the receptionist the remaining bag of fudge to thank her for her discretion. She accepted it gratefully and asked if there was anything else she could do for me. I thanked her but told her no, then rushed upstairs to stuff all of my belongings into my bag. There wasn't much – enough for a new life and little more.

The problem was I heard Jason's voice in every little move I made.

'You don't look like you used to.'

'I've had better-looking women than you.'

'Wow, you really let yourself go.'

I fought to keep tears out of my eyes, stuffing the folded clothes in as compactly as possible. My teeth grinding, I zipped up my case and got the hell out of there, rushing down to the lobby while working up a sweat. I had this insane fear that I would bump into him at any minute, and there would be no coming back from that. How would I even explain myself, much less get away from him without him hurting me?

Downstairs, I breezed past reception and went for the door. I stopped there, realising I would no longer be safe once reaching the street. There were ways around this, however, and it started with me heading back to the young receptionist.

'Is everything okay?' she asked, putting down the phone with a concerned frown.

'What taxi service do you use here?'

'A-Plus. A local company.'

'If I use them and that man comes back...'

'They won't tell anyone where you went.'

'How can you be so sure?'

'It's my uncle's company. I'll ask him to be discreet.'

I let out a relieved smile and thanked her, then took a seat as she picked the phone back up and ordered a taxi. From the way she explained the situation, it sounded like her uncle had picked up. I watched her, incredibly grateful for her help and even seeing small parts of a younger me in her. Before Jason got to me and killed my spirit, that was.

'Did you fall out of the ugly tree?'

'You're not pretty enough to be this boring.'

'Would it kill you to smile from time to time?'

I instantly rose and approached the desk. It wouldn't surprise me if she was starting to get annoyed with me, but she didn't show it in the slightest. In fact, the only vibe she gave off was one of warmth and security. I trusted her, which was why I asked the question...

'Am I ugly?'

The young lady froze, studying me. 'Excuse me?'

'Just... from the perspective of a young woman, do you think I'm ugly?'

'Not at all. Actually, I think you're beautiful. Why do you ask?'

'Never mind. Thank you. For everything.'

I never saw that lady again, but I'd never forget her. As soon as the taxi came, I climbed in and asked him to take me to the neighbouring village. Then, as I sat there in silence and thought about everything Jason had said to make me feel anything less than gorgeous, I finally made up my mind that it was time for a change.

No longer would I have this weak chin. I would say goodbye to the nose I'd hated my entire life. My ears could go back with just a small surgery, and my more youthful looks might return. Perhaps I would even look better than before, rising out of the ashes of my failed relationship like the phoenix. That was what I needed for my self-confidence.

But that wasn't the only reason. The more I changed my face, the less I would look like myself. If I were to spend the foreseeable future on the run from that bastard, it might help to be less recognisable. I found this concept appealing – a solid theory to back up the decision that had already been made. All I needed was to find a good surgeon I could trust.

And the confidence to commit to this plan.

Chapter 8
Daisy, Now

NIGHT HAS COME AND GONE. Not that I slept much. My body won't even start to relax, and my mind isn't much better. I can't seem to let go of the fact that I'm stuck in a stranger's spare bedroom and there's no way out.

Believe me, I've tried.

Lying here on the bed long after the sun has risen, I think back to when Cillian locked the door. I rushed over and banged as hard as possible, screaming at the top of my lungs to let me out. The only thing I ever heard back was him telling me not to exert myself, right before his footsteps pounded down the hall and faded into silence.

My heart broke right then and there, faced with the reality of my situation.

Sighing, I shift position on the bed to stop my back from hurting, then replay the following events in my head. I remember running to the window next (as anyone with half a brain would do) and thanked the stars above that there were no bars behind the glass.

Unfortunately, that wasn't enough.

Opening the window, I peered down at the ground below. I never did understand metrics too well, but let's just say there was no way of surviving a jump like that. In the best-case scenario, I might break a plethora of bones and scream to high heaven. Even if that didn't alert Cillian, how the hell was I supposed to make it out of there?

Hobbling, that was how.

In short, jumping was not an option.

Neither was climbing.

Ever since then, I've had nothing to do but lie here and rethink my life. There's a slight chance it's not as bad as it seems – Cillian might come and let me out any second now, apologise for ever having locked me in here, then send me on my merry way. It's a daydream, of course, but what else is there to do in here but watch TV or read?

And I'm definitely not in the mood for either of those. For all I know, I'll be dead in a day or two.

That's how much he scares me.

Every muscle in my body tenses up when I hear him come and go. It's happened so many times now – like he's checking on me – but he doesn't say a word before disappearing again. I glance at the clock and see it's almost lunchtime, and he hasn't even brought me any food. Something has shifted in that man. The kindness is gone, and it's plain to see he has no intention of looking after me any further.

So then, what does he want from me?

I'm too scared to even think about it. Given how my relationship with Jason turned out, it's safe to say I've endured enough abuse to last a lifetime. If Cillian, the last man I'll ever trust, does anything to hurt me, then I'll probably just be better off dead.

But no, I can't let my fighting spirit leave me. I must stay strong, no matter how hopeless it seems. Even now, as I listen to Cillian's footsteps grow quieter once again, wrapping my arms around my growling stomach, one thing is dead clear.

I can't give up.

I have to escape.

BELIEVE ME, a thousand different plans have run through my head. I'd like to say at least one of them sounds hopeful, but that would be a big, fat lie. There are really only three options anyway: make that dreaded leap of faith, wait it out and pray someone comes to visit the property, or beg Cillian to let me out.

My mind is made up.

It's another couple of hours before he makes his next appearance. My stomach is rumbling so hard it feels as though it's been punched, and my lips are bone dry. It seems my surgeon's aftercare ended the moment he locked me in here, so it's a good thing I intend to grovel.

As the footsteps draw nearer, I swing my legs off the bed and hurry across the room. There's a small gap under the door where I can see his shadow pass, so I start thumping against the wood until my knuckles are sore. Naturally, my inclination is to curse him with every name under the sun, but that's not going to work.

I need to suck up to him.

'Cillian, are you there? I'm so, so sorry for how I behaved.'

There's no sound coming from the other side of the door. I wonder if he even heard me. He must have, because the shadow is still there, so why isn't he saying anything? The silence is enough to drive a woman crazy, and it just might.

'I don't like you snooping,' he finally says. His voice is unsettlingly calm, as if nothing at all has happened. As if this is a natural, everyday occurrence for him. It does lead me to wonder... has he ever done this to somebody else?

'That's understandable,' I say, matching his smooth tone. 'I apologise for that.'

'Why did you do it?'

'Curiosity, maybe.'

'Did you find what you were looking for?'

The phone. That's what he must be thinking of. It feels like he's trying to trip me up – to make me admit that I was specifically looking for it. Not that it should matter either way, considering he must have taken it from me a while ago, but it's better to play into his palm right now. It's time to swallow my pride and press on.

'I wasn't looking for anything in particular. It's just that this house is so beautiful, and it made me want to explore every inch of it. I found the phone by accident, and I suppose it made me panic that something weird was going on. You're not the type of person to just steal someone's property – that's obvious – so I'm really sorry for freaking out.'

'Yes, I'm not a thief.'

'Exactly.'

'Or a creep, if that's why you wanted to run from me.'

'Definitely not a creep.' Even thinking my next words is enough to make me feel disgusting. 'Actually, you're the kindest man I've ever met. You let me stay here for free, feed me, take care of me, and my reaction to finding the phone was just shameful. I don't know if you can ever forgive me, but I'd love to go back to how things were.'

There's that pause again. Long. Agonising. It feels like I've fallen into a bottomless pit, condemned to an eternity of silence while knowing there's no way out. I'm starting to think he's gone back down the hall when he finally speaks again.

'You'll try to run away,' he says.

'No.'

'How can I trust you?'

'The same way I trusted you.'

Another pause. Then...

'Daisy, you're as smart as you are beautiful, but that will change when your recovery is over. I would like to keep you here long enough to see your results, but that will take weeks. There's no way you'll spend that amount of time here without trying to leave.'

'You're wrong,' I plead. 'Do I actually *want* to be here? Not any more – not really. But I can make my peace with it as long as I have free roam of the house. Monitor me all you like. Follow me into every room if you must. But locking me in here and expecting me to enjoy it is a fool's dream. And you're no fool, are you?'

There it was. Honesty with a dash of bluff. I can tell Cillian is thinking about it, his throat making a soft humming sound as if he's mulling it over. It must be refreshing for him to hear something so raw and honest (as long as he believes it), so that's playing in my favour.

After a short while, there's a clunking sound in the lock. The door pops open, and the hinge whines. I fight every temptation to rush at this man, but he's already proven his strength and power over me. This is something I'll have to do calmly, methodically.

That is, if I want to have any hope of survival.

Cillian is grinning like a devious devil when the door is fully open. He's wearing a turtleneck, and I'm jealous of his collar just because it gets to strangle him. I shrink back, knowing full well that he could end me right now if he chooses to. Except from the glint in his eye, it seems like his guard has fallen just a little.

'Come,' he says. 'Let's have a spot of lunch.'

I follow him because there's nothing else to do and because I'll need the food. It's been a long time since I've eaten, and my body is weak. It's craving the energy, not just to fuel itself for the rest of the day but for the workout it's about to receive.

It needs the energy to run.

IT'S FUNNY; when I'm not being dragged up the stairs by my hair and thrown into a room where he keeps me as a prisoner for hours on end, Cillian is actually pretty good to me.

I explained just how hungry I was, and he quickly decided to turn a light lunch into a full feast. Although he admitted to hardly preparing much of the food by himself, he scribbled down a list of my favourite foods, tossed them into the air fryer, then presented me with sausages, waffles, and eggs and dished it up with a fruit salad. I wolfed it down so quickly I made a mess every-where, and during that time, a thought hit me like lightning.

He doesn't prepare his own food.

That means somebody else does it for him.

That means somebody else comes to the house.

I make a mental note of that but still intend to run. It's just a matter of choosing my timing. I set my plan into motion by telling him I'd like to sit in the living room. It's the room closest to the front door, and the wall that runs alongside it is made entirely of glass. I stare at it a little too long as we go inside, which is where Cillian stops me dead in my tracks.

'See something you like?' he asks.

'Yes.' I nod beyond the glass. 'That's a nice pool you have.'

'It's not just nice – it's beautiful – but you can't go out there.'

'Why not?'

Cillian points at my masked face, a silent reminder that I'm still recovering from my surg-eries. As if that's not enough, he adds, 'No exercise whatsoever for six weeks, and certainly no getting the nose cast wet. You have been avoiding it when showering, correct?'

'Correct.'

'Good. You can swim when the cast comes off.'

'How long will that take?'

'A while longer.'

I nod again, then take a seat and let my eyes soak up everything in the bright, airy room. I don't really give a rat's brown arsehole about the swimming pool, but it's important I throw Cillian off the scent that I'm about to make a run for it. Patience is the key, of course, so I continue looking around the room at the high oak beams, the gorgeous marble fireplace, and the TV that covers an entire cobblestone wall.

'Could I trouble you for a glass of water?' I ask.

'Of course you can.'

The kitchen is right next to the living room, and he'll only take a minute. We both know that's not enough time to run, so I'm using it to show that he can trust me – that if he leaves me alone, then I won't move so much as an inch. When he returns, I make a fuss of how grateful I am, down the water, then ask to watch a little TV. He's quick to show off his surround sound, then hits a button that brings the blinds down and darkens the entire room. Before I know it, we're watching an episode of

Dexter. Believe it or not, I've gone off serial killer stories.

It cuts a little too close to the bone.

When the episode finishes, I lie and explain how much I love the show. Cillian agrees that it's good and promises it will get even better with each episode. I've actually already seen the whole thing twice, but my arse-kissing skills are at their peak. I entertain my captor just a short while longer before touching a hand to my stomach.

'What's wrong, darling?' he asks.

I try not to throw up at being called that, then employ the next part of my plan.

'I know that was a lot to eat, but I'm actually still hungry. Is there any chance...'

'You want more food?'

'Something light. If that's okay?'

Cillian smiles. A few days ago, it would have charmed me. Now, I'm sickened by it. 'What can I get for you?' he asks. 'You name it, it's yours. As long as we have it in the house.'

'Anything at all?'

'Within reason.'

'Do you have any rice cakes?' I know he has even before he nods. 'What I'd really love is four of those. Two with cream cheese and strawberries, two with peanut butter and sliced banana. Perhaps a coffee to go with it?'

Cillian knocks his head back and laughs. 'Interesting choices. I'm pretty sure I can accommodate, although the coffee will still have to be decaf. Because...' He taps his chin and then points to mine. 'Give me a minute.'

As he leaves, I know it will be more than a minute. I deliberately chose food that will require slicing and spreading and a lot of fuss. The more sophisticated the snack, the longer he will take. The longer he takes, the more time I have to get out the front door.

Just in case he's figured me out, I wait a minute before heading for the door. Then, I get up nervously and tread as lightly as possible out of the room. The door is just a few feet away, the kitchen doorway not much farther from that. Cillian's shadow glides across the floor. All it will take to be seen is for him to lean a little to his left.

All it will take to escape is for me to run.

It's now or never. As a shiver slides up my spine, I shudder and run for the door. My bare feet barely make a sound on the carpet. I'm watching the kitchen as I reach the door, so close I can almost taste it. My hand goes straight for the handle, and of course, it's locked. But I remember seeing him put the key on top of the door frame, so I reach for it immediately and—

'Gone,' I say so quietly I'm unsure if it was just a thought.

All hope drains from me. My body goes weak, my shoulders slump. Cillian must have known what I had planned, and why should I be so surprised? He's a smart man – smart enough to become a surgeon in the first place – so why did I ever think I could outsmart him?

I brought this on myself, I realise as I tread lightly back into the living room. I'm trapped in this house in the middle of nowhere, and my only hope of escape is either through smashing the long, glass wall and making a run for it or waiting to see if anyone will come to the house. Considering how slow I am at running, even when I'm wearing shoes, my mind is made up.

There's no way out. At least not at the moment.

Right now, I officially belong to Cillian.

Chapter 9
Daisy, Now

THE REST of that day was spent hanging around with the man I couldn't tolerate. Even looking at him made me feel sick inside, so spending the whole afternoon in his living room and wondering how the hell I was going to escape only made me more anxious.

Today is a new day, however. It feels a little odd to wake up knowing the door isn't locked – I can get up, walk around, maybe even start looking for that damn key. It does make me wonder though... has he set up some kind of alarm? Cillian is a paranoid type, and he knows I want to get out of here as soon as possible. I can just imagine him sitting by the front door with a shotgun on his lap, like an old man in the Wild West. Only instead of keeping someone out, he's ensuring someone stays in.

I'm trying to act normal, at least. Cillian hasn't said anything about my escape attempt yesterday, but why should he? I barely did anything at the door, my dreams of going home – wherever that is – completely squashed. Unless he saw me feeling around for the key, there's nothing to complain about. No reason for him to hurt me...

Cillian catches me at the dining table between mouthfuls of cereal. The way he hovers in the doorway gives me the creeps, but I offer a thin, milky smile, then look away. The less I have to look at that eerie son of a bitch, the better.

'We need to talk,' he says.

'What about?'

'Yesterday.'

I instantly panic so much that I'm worried heat has flushed to my face. Can he see how concerned he makes me? Will that affect his opinion of me and the way he treats me? It's impossible not to look at him... even if just to make sure he's not rushing at me.

'What about yesterday?' I ask, dropping my spoon and pushing away the empty bowl.

'You know exactly what.'

'Did I do something wrong?'

'What do *you* think?'

I pause before answering, uncertain if he's referring to my pathetic escape attempt or something else entirely. It's not long before I realise it's best to be honest but tactical about my wording. 'You mean... the fact I wanted to get out of the house?'

Cillian steps inside. I turn to face him, and he's grinning from ear to ear. 'Precisely that.' He drags out a chair and sits beside me. 'If you so very badly want to leave, all you have to do is ask. It's not like you're a prisoner here.'

A hopeful fire ignites within me. 'Really?'

'Of course. You're free to come and go as you please.'

'What about getting back into town?'

Cillian raises an eyebrow. 'Why would you go into town?'

'Because... you just said I could leave...?'

'Yes, you can go right now if you like.'

'Right now?' I repeat for clarity. 'I can walk out that door?'

'Oh, Daisy, you do make me laugh.' Cillian snickers like a villain in some old cartoon, then shakes his head. 'You can walk out that door whenever you like. It's just best I go with you to ensure you don't exert yourself. Then, when we get back, we can have a nice lunch.'

Before I can protest, he's on his feet and rushing to get our coats. My heart sinks into my belly as it suddenly becomes clear what he really meant. He wasn't saying I could leave this house forever – he was simply suggesting I could go and get some air at anytime. But when he returns with our coats and an almost excited smile, it's so very easy to see...

He'll never let me go alone.

———

WE DON'T GO TOO FAR, and I imagine that's how he wanted it.

But at least the walk itself is pleasant. There's one long path that stretches on as far as the eye can see. Its background is a clear blue sky with only a slight threat of grey clouds on the horizon. The stone pathway is bordered by two narrow ditches, and beyond those are luscious green fields with poppies and a splash of yellow brightening the scenery. The air is so warm that we haven't even put on our jackets.

It's funny though – even with all of that, it's still impossible to feel positive.

'How's your face feeling right now?' Cillian asks at my side.

I can't bear to look at him, even if the compression garment does disguise my anger-heated cheeks. 'It's feeling okay. My chin feels swollen, and my ears hurt, but I can't wait to get this stupid cast off my nose. I can hardly breathe.'

It's true. I've spent the past couple of days fighting the urge to sneeze (apparently, I'm not allowed to do that unless it's through my mouth, which is gross). Breathing is difficult at the best of times, and the pollen in the air isn't helping.

'That can come off in two or three days,' he says, his voice dry and monotone.

'Really? So soon?'

'Would you rather wait?'

'Definitely not.'

A quick glance tells me he's smiling, but it's a thin, forced smile. We continue walking, the only sounds that of the chirping birds and our footsteps scuffing along the stones as we go. I feel highly uncomfortable, like I want to run but could never get away with it. Even at my peak health, Cillian has to be faster than me.

He's certainly stronger – he already proved that.

As the walk goes on, I have a quick look back over my shoulder to see how far we've come. It's far enough that I'm ready to turn back. Even if it is going to be another ten or fifteen minutes before we return to the house. I just feel so irritable.

That's to be expected when you can hardly breathe.

'Is something the matter?' Cillian asks.

'No. Just wondering how far we are from the house.'

'Why is that important?'

'It's not. I'm simply curious.'

'There's no need to be.'

If not from the tone in his voice, it's easy to see I've upset him simply from the change in my mood. I tend to have an instinct for these things – take it from a woman who recently spent a large chunk of her relationship treading on eggshells.

'Have I done something wrong?' I dare to ask.

'What do *you* think?'

'If I have, it was unintentional.'

'Hmm.' Cillian clears his throat. 'It usually is, isn't it?'

'What?'

'Unintentional. When you piss me off.'

A silence forms. It's not a comfortable one. I try to ignore it, walking onwards and seeing if he'd consider sweeping it under the rug. We make it all of ten metres before Cillian stops in his tracks and says my name. I stop, turning around with my heart racing.

'Are you always going to be this paranoid?' he asks.

Me? What about you? I think but don't say. Instead, I go for: 'No, I didn't mean to—'

'You're too inquisitive, Daisy. It's incredibly frustrating.'

'How can I change that?'

'Stop asking questions.'

'But I didn't... I mean...' It's time to resign. 'I'm really sorry.'

Cillian's face droops into disappointment. My pulse quickens. The silence grows, and every second that passes drains a little more hope that this isn't going to be another angry flare-up. I can feel it in the air like cats can sense storms from miles away.

'It's time we head home,' he says flatly.

'Agreed.'

His steely blue eyes rise to meet mine. 'You *agree*? Why is that, exactly?'

I must choose my words carefully because anything I say could easily set him off. It's like his patience is a pool of oil, and my voice is the spark. Heat flushing through my aching head, I speak very clearly, very slowly, and oh-so hopelessly.

'It's just been a long day.'

Cillian smirks, but it's false. 'How? It's still the morning.'

'But the pain is—'

'Better than most people have it.'

'What do you mean?'

'You know what, Daisy?' He storms towards me as I flinch. 'You're a bloody ungrateful woman. Not only did you have three highly successful surgeries in one day, but you have some of the best aftercare in the world, free boarding in a beautiful home, and the kind of company most women would kill for.'

It's not what he's saying that freaks me out, but the word he used.

Kill.

'What do you want me to say?' I ask, feeling his breath on my barely exposed face.

'You mean you can't think for yourself?'

'I just don't want to upset you.'

'It's a little late for that,' he snaps.

My head cocks back. 'Whatever I did to upset you.'

'Whatever you did?' Cillian shakes his head in sheer disappointment. '*Whatever you did?* One of these days, you're going to look around and realise just how good you have it. It won't be anytime soon, but it will definitely happen. Then, when you've finally learned a little bit of gratitude, we just might be able to stay under the same roof without you winding me up every five bloody minutes!'

With that, he turns on his heel and marches back down the long path towards the house. I think about using this opportunity to run, but I still doubt I'll make it. Even if I could outrun him, we're miles from the nearest town, and I don't even know which one. Then, *if* I got there safely, there's no way of knowing whether he'll still find me.

As if reading my thoughts, Cillian turns from a few metres down the path.

'Are you coming or not?' he snaps.

Like a blind sheep, I follow my shepherd back towards my prison.

It's not like I have a choice, is it?

NATURALLY, the rest of the day is painfully uncomfortable.

Cillian sweeps through the rooms in an awful mood, directionless, almost as if he wants me to ask about it. There's no way I'm going to open up that conversation. Not when my safety is in the hands of this emotionally unstable control freak.

Instead, I settle down with a book that my eyes keep skimming over. The words aren't really going in, and it takes ten minutes per page. It's just an excuse, really – something to make it look like I shouldn't and cannot be disturbed.

I spend most of that time thinking about Lily. About what happened to her and why she hasn't contacted me yet? I'd ask her if I had my phone, which I don't – that belongs to Cillian now, and I don't have the balls to ask for it back.

Later into the evening, when my hay fever has died down and I'm lying in bed just to stare mindlessly at the ceiling, there's a gentle rap at my door. I sit up quickly, pulling the blanket over my body for no other reason than to cover myself that little bit more.

'Hello?' I say meekly.

Cillian's bashful face appears in the small gap of the doorway. 'Can we talk?'

'What about?'

'Earlier.'

'Fine.'

He comes in as if it's my home and he's the guest. I don't mind the change of power in the room – it's refreshing and sort of comforting. It's only a slight feeling, but I feel safe enough as he pulls out a chair and sits beside the bed, his elbows on his knees and his chin resting on his cupped hands. His dazzling eyes bore into me.

'My behaviour earlier was inexcusable,' he says calmly.

'Oh, don't worry about—'

His raised hand cuts me off. 'Do not make excuses for me. You're merely a guest in my home and have done nothing wrong. The words I choose and the way I express them are not appropriate. I'd like to make an effort to change that, if you will only give me a chance.'

It's hard to tell if this is some kind of trap. After carefully considering a handful of responses, I eventually settle for a nod and a soft smile. Cillian watches me longer, as if waiting for more. With nothing of importance left to say, I stumble to fill the silence.

'Please relax,' I say. 'None of it struck me personally.'

Cillian matches my smile. 'You're not upset?'

'Not at all?'

'So we can start over?'

'Definitely.'

As he gets up to leave, a feeling of relief washes over me. It's always nice to hear someone apologise, even if it is hard to believe they won't do it again. But Cillian seems sincere in his apology – his pleading for forgiveness. While I watch him restore the chair to its previous position and then head for the door, I start to feel like everything is going to be okay.

And then he speaks.

'I'm glad we could make this work,' he says as he opens the door. Then, with one swift comment, he sucks all the hope and positivity out of my body, replacing it with nothing but ice-cold fear and dread for the coming days. 'You're the best girlfriend I ever had.'

Cillian leaves and closes the door.

All I feel is shock.

Chapter 10
Daisy, Then

The taxi driver stopped outside a small village shop that sat on the corner of a narrow and crooked street. The windows were boarded up, there was a patchwork of missing-persons posters half torn on the wall, and a group of youths who looked like troublemakers loitered on the corner. It looked like I had fallen from heaven and landed right in the depths of hell.

'You can pay by card if you need to,' the driver said bluntly.

'This is *it*?'

'The whole village, yeah.'

Nothing had ever felt so daunting. I'd been staring out the window as we drove through, and believe me when I say this shop was the only attraction in these slums. I wouldn't have felt safe staying there, and I didn't even know how I'd fill my time if I did.

'How far to the next village?' I asked.

'Couple of hours. It's more like a town than a village though.'

'Does it have hotels?'

'Probably.'

'Take me there, please.'

'It'll cost you.'

The driver didn't even see me shrug before he pulled off and started speeding through the horrible little lanes. I sat back and rubbed my temples, feeling around my face and knowing it was due to change soon. To be honest, I felt bad about having to do it, but the idea was sort of exciting. I thought it would be fun to look completely different.

Not long later, we drove through a large town that looked a lot cleaner. People were walking around in half-decent clothes – some of them suits – as we passed by letting agents, supermarkets, banks, and bakeries. It seemed to be thriving, and I felt a lot better about staying in a place like this for a night or two.

Anything to get away from *him*.

After paying the hefty taxi fare, I checked in at a Travelodge, dumped my bag, then went for a wander. I kept catching my reflection in shop windows, cringing at the sight of my face. It was going to cost a fortune to change all of these features, so I started to consider choosing the most defining elements and weighing up the price. My nose would be the first thing to go – not only had I hated it since I was a kid, but it would change the whole shape of my face. This bulky, crooked thing stuck out like a sore thumb. I did consider changing my ears, but that would have been a more minor surgery that would still leave me recognisable.

Priorities, priorities.

I had time to think about it. It wasn't as if I'd even chosen a surgeon yet, much less had a consultation. I had to take my mind off it for now, stopping at shop windows and giving thought to what I'd look like in the outfits displayed on the mannequins. Perhaps I didn't need to change my face, I thought. Maybe a nice haircut and a change of clothes would suffice.

Then, as if to derail this delusion, I heard the laughter behind me.

I turned in a split second, mostly out of curiosity. There were three of them, two teenage girls sitting on the bench and a slender, dark-skinned boy about the same age who had his foot up on the bench. They were all looking my way with humour in their eyes. When I stared a little too long, they chuckled. One of them snorted as she laughed.

Feeling paranoid that they were laughing at me, I turned my back on them and admired the outfit in the window once more. Then, there was mumbling behind me. I saw from the reflection in the glass that they were getting up. My body tensed. I prepared to defend myself. They came my way, and I glanced around to see if there were witnesses.

There were plenty.

'Fall out of the ugly tree, did you?' the boy said.

'Hit every branch on the way down,' one of the girls added.

They all laughed again and moved on. The danger had passed, but the lasting effect of their words kick-started my wishes again. Just when I'd thought I could live with the way I looked, the cruelty of others had knocked me back down. I was getting sick and tired of people treating me like this. I longed for a better life – one where people would treat me nicer, even if it was based simply on my appearance. Was that so much to ask for?

Heartbroken, I moved on from the shop window.

In the opposite direction from those kids, of course.

———

THE TOWN WASN'T so bad – I could commit to staying here just a little while longer, especially if he was hot on my trail. The longer I stayed put and hid in the anonymity of this obscure little town, the more chance there was of him moving farther away from me on his hunt.

Yes, it was a moment to relax amid all the chaos of leaving Jason. This meant I should probably shop for some supplies – a few bottles of water, cheap store-bought sandwiches in case hunger came for me in the hotel room, and a book or two to keep me occupied while I hid. I felt like a fugitive, running from my inevitable capture.

If I wasn't so scared, I might have even found it a little exciting.

'You must be new in town.'

The voice startled me while at the checkout of a Tesco Express. I whirled around to find a little old lady with oversized glasses and grey curls that did nothing for the shape of her face. But who was I to judge – I wasn't exactly an oil painting.

'What do you mean?' I asked, wondering if I was really that obvious.

'You're paying full price for those sandwiches.'

'Shouldn't I?'

'Everyone around here knows they reduce them to half price in about an hour.' She pointed a wrinkled, veiny hand at an empty refrigerator on the far wall, where a small table with a pricing gun awaited its use. 'Wait over there and save yourself some money.'

Smiling politely, I shook my head. 'Thank you, but I'm in a rush.'

'Oh, take life slowly. Trust me. I'm Sue, by the way.'

A fake name fell out of my mouth so fast I don't even remember what it was. It was just enough to keep her happy, pay for my sandwiches, then haul the couple of carrier bags out of there with only a curt nod for a goodbye. I thought about that the whole way home.

Why was I so scared to give my real name?

Why didn't I want to leave the hotel room for too long?

What was my actual destination?

Would I be forever on the run?

It bothered me that I didn't have an answer to a single one of these questions. I carried that burden like a looming, murky cloud all the way back to the hotel. God even knows what I was going to do with the rest of the day – I was too focused on thinking of it as a retreat.

An *escape*.

Not that it did me any favours – that gloomy cloud cracked above me like a thunderclap the second I walked through those hotel doors. I heard him before I saw him, but only by a fraction of a second. Just a moment long enough to feel my body shudder with terror.

There he was.

In the hotel.

Standing at the front desk and showing the receptionist a photo of me on his phone. I couldn't even see his face, but it was definitely him. I stood there, frozen, torn between running upstairs or out the front door. As salty sweat rolled down my temple in warm beads, I raced towards the hallway, practically smacking the key card against the lock. Before I knew it, I was darting down the corridor towards my hotel room, dropping the carrier bags and focusing on the

only thing that was important to me at that moment.

Packing my things, then getting the hell out of there.

I COULDN'T BELIEVE he'd found me.

How?!

Perhaps I just wasn't as smart as I thought – all that careful preparation and planning, all that carefully decisive thinking on where he could and would go just to find me. I'd really thought he would never come to this town. A town I'd never even heard of until shortly before arriving. Just how exactly was that possible?

That's all that ran through my mind in crazy, spinning circles while I threw my bag on to the bed and stuffed my things into it. There wasn't much to pack – just some cosmetics and a toothbrush. I didn't even care about all the stuff I'd bought but had to leave behind.

All I wanted was to get out of there.

As soon as I grabbed my bag, my shirt clung to me with cold sweat. I headed for the door in a hurry, reaching for the handle but stopping only when the hotel phone rang. Heart pounding, I froze, wondering if I should answer and settle my anxiety or simply go and never look back. Neither seemed like a sensible option, but I couldn't deal with an unanswered phone.

So I crossed the room and answered it.

'Yes?' I asked in a wavering voice.

'Mrs. Campbell?' a soft, delicate voice confirmed.

'Speaking.'

'There's a gentleman here who would like to speak with you.'

That voice faded into my subconscious as I dived deep into thought. Was he listening to this phone call from the other side of the desk? Was she confirming out loud that I was in this hotel right now? The panic made me shaky. I didn't know what to do.

'Mrs. Campbell?' she said, dragging me back to the moment. 'Are you there?'

'I'm here, yes.'

'Should I send him up?'

'No, definitely not. I don't want him anywhere near me.'

A brief pause, then a whisper. 'Are you in danger?'

'Possibly.'

'Should I call security? Perhaps the police?'

God no, I thought. Anything but the police. Although security might be helpful...

'Could you have security distract him for a few minutes? I would like to check out and sneak through the back door if possible. Can I just leave my key in the room and get out of here? Please?'

The most soothing, calming voice told me it would be no problem whatsoever, and she even offered to refund my night's stay based on the lack of safety provided by the hotel. I gratefully accepted, hung up the phone, then waited a moment before heading downstairs.

Once more, my shock and terror seized me as I headed down the hall. He was right there, being escorted through a door by a member of security. The guard was dressed all in black and had a fierce demeanour about him, but even he was dwarfed by my pursuer. In that moment, it felt like nothing and nobody could keep me safe.

I waited, my mouth dry and hands clammy until they passed through the door and vanished from sight. The exit door was beyond that, and it took all of my courage to pass it. I expected them to come out at any minute, right in front of my face.

Every step brought me closer to dropping to my knees, giving up on the idea of my new life.

My *safe* life.

But it never happened. I made it through, and nobody stood in my way.

Bursting through the exit door, I slung the bag strap over my shoulder and got the hell out of there as fast as I could. There was no telling where my next taxi would take me. All I knew was that he was behind me, so I would go to the far ends of the earth just to get away from him.

As if that would work.

It hadn't so far.

Chapter 11
Daisy, Now

So, Cillian thinks I'm his girlfriend.

It's certainly not ideal, is it?

I'm trying to remain calm, but...

What the hell is going on in his head?!

It's something I've been trying to process for a couple of days now, playing it safe and not so much as looking at the front door while he's around. I also wonder how long he's going to take to kiss me. If he truly thinks we're a couple, surely he would have done it by now? And the cruel irony of it is, if he hadn't turned out to be a controlling nutcase, he's somebody I probably would have been attracted to in the first place. I mean, why not; he's handsome, has money, is successful, and he has height on his side.

What's not to like?

Save for his loose-cannon attitude and egomania, that is.

I've been spending a lot of time in my room. Mostly to get away from Cillian, but a smaller reason is that it's just nice to rest. The compression garment is starting to hurt my neck – I take it off here or there, knowing that soon enough, I'll only have to wear it at night. That's the same day the cast will come off my nose, and I've never yearned for a day so badly.

Except the day I can get the hell out of here.

There's movement downstairs. Cillian seems to be enjoying his time off, piano music playing softly from a vinyl player downstairs. It's quite pleasant, actually, soothing for the most part, but would be making me a little anxious if the door wasn't there to cushion the volume.

But that's not the only sound. There's something outside. Something that has me on my bare feet and crossing the room in a hurry. My forehead almost strikes the glass as I peer out the window with all the excitement of a young girl at Christmas.

I'm sure I know that sound.

I watch the driveway, looking for it. My heart

drops, and then so does my previously lit-up expression. I should have known it was too good to be true. I'm just about to chastise myself for being so naïve, slinking away from the window with the bitter taste of disappointment.

Then another noise.

A confirmation.

A hopeful breath escapes me. I stare out of the window again, pushing hard against the glass to reach the most obscure angle. That's when I see it, clear as day. A glimmer of hope. A very dim light in the dark, distant expanse that is my bleak future.

There's a car parked in front of the house.

We have a visitor.

I watch with joy as a lady steps out. From the little I can see, she's a relatively short woman in her fifties. Olive skin, speckles of grey in her tied-up hair. She steps along the crunchy gravel to the back of the car, where she pulls something out and carries it in both hands. I'm squinting right up until I figure out what it is.

A bucket of cleaning supplies.

Of course, I think, grinning from ear to ear. *Cillian has a cleaner.*

My heart and soul full of hope, I spring across the room and reach for some jeans to wear. Kicking off my pyjama bottoms so Cillian won't get to see me all cosy, I step into the denim and think about what I'm going to say. That woman can help me – I just know she can. She has a car, which means she has the freedom to come and go. All I have to do is let her know I'm stuck here, ask her to call the police. She can get far away from here before even having to make the call, so it's not like she's even putting herself at risk.

But she'll need to be alone when I approach.

It shouldn't be a problem, I accept while going for the door.

But what happens next is.

At first, I think the handle is stuck – that maybe the wood has swollen in the heat. No such thing, I realise as I use both hands to tug harder. Then, while all my hopes crash and burn, I drop to my knees and peer through the crevasse in the door frame. I see the gold-plated lock taking up the space. A clear indicator that I'm going nowhere.

Cillian must have thought this through.

He's locked me in here on purpose.

Again.

I SIT BY THE DOOR, like a dog longing for its master.

But I'm not waiting for my master.

I'm waiting for his cleaner.

The side of the chest of drawers supports my back. A cushion beneath my backside softens the pain from the floor. Sweat mats hair to my forehead while I listen hopefully in the dead silence. The cleaner – maid, whatever she is – must come down to this end of the house.

Eventually.

Two hours pass. My stomach is starting to make sounds, and Cillian hasn't even come to see me. He'd usually be offering me food every thirty minutes or bringing me a refill of water, but there's nothing. Although I *can* hear the gentle mumble of his voice above the piano jazz emanating from downstairs. If only the volume changed to indicate the distance.

Then I could see if there's progress.

Finally, minutes later, there are footsteps. I rush to lie on my front and look through the gap under the door. I'm waiting to see feet – confirmation that someone is outside – before I even dare to speak out loud. What if I tried too soon and only then realise it's Cillian I'm talking to? Imagine that:

I'm begging my own captor to save me from him. I shudder to even think how he'd react to such a thing, but it definitely wouldn't be good.

The word 'violent' springs to mind.

Shadows drift along the floor. My neck hurts as I crane it to see. They pass by swiftly, with no way of telling if they belong to Cillian or the maid. It occurs to me then that there will never be a way of knowing for sure, so there are only really two options.

Ask for help.

Or don't.

Well, screw hanging around in this baking-hot bedroom all day and praying for salvation. I was never close with my father, but he once told me that things only happen if you make them. He wasn't right about much, but that was one of his finer moments.

I wait for the right moment – when the shadows glide along the hallway floor again. As soon as they do, I pound against the wood and shout for help. The shadows stop. The *feet* stop. Then I climb up and stand, leaning against the door so hard I'm basically hugging it.

'Hello?' I say, desperation cracking in my voice like a timid wave against a rock.

Nothing.

'Is somebody out there? I really need your help. Cillian locked me in here.'

Silence again.

Then a shuffle.

'Cillian?' A weak voice. Feminine. A thick accent from... somewhere.

'Yes, Cillian. Your boss. My captor. He has me locked in here against my will.'

'Help?' she says.

'Help, yes, please. Call the police or something.'

'Policía?'

She's Spanish, then, I think. From the very little I know about languages. But that's okay. The only three words she needs to know have already reached her ears: Cillian, help, police. All the ingredients to make a nice big freedom pie.

But she hasn't spoken in a few long, painful seconds. I wait in the silence, praying for liberation. Is she weighing up her options? Processing the language? Perhaps Cillian has come upstairs and she doesn't want to make it obvious that she's found me. Any of these are better than the obvious alternative, made evident by another shuffle of feet.

She's moving on.

'No,' I gasp, dropping to my belly again. Pain rips up my neck as I look under the door. The shadows are gone. The *maid* is gone and, with her, my only chance of getting out of here. Now, all I can do is retire to the bed and hold myself, wishing I could turn back the clock and wait a little longer for Lily to come pick me up.

Where are you? I ask as if she can hear me and answer.

But she can't, and she never will. Lily isn't coming for me either. Nobody is.

I'm probably here forever.

Or until I die.

THE MAID LEFT HOURS AGO. Watching her leave was like watching a life jacket float out to sea, carried on the vicious waves. I was stranded. Alone. My bed was an island as the sun dipped behind the horizon, chased by the night.

The room is pitch-black two hours after that. The house is silent. I've listened carefully the entire time, hoping beyond hope that the car would come back or that the maid has contacted the police to help me. But the truth is, I still don't know if she told Cillian what she heard. The fact he hasn't come by to punish me yet makes me thank God for small miracles.

The last thing I need is to be punished.

Soft footsteps patter up the hallway now. I feel my body tense before the sound even properly registers. That's how afraid of him I am – how desperately I want to leave this house and go back to... well, not my old life, but maybe a new one.

The lock clunks. The door swings open. Cillian peers inside and then flicks a switch that floods the room with harsh light. I cover my eyes, and he dims it, then comes inside. Adjusting to the brightness, I remove my hand and hug the same pillow I've been hugging this whole time. As far as I'm concerned, this pillow is my only friend in the world.

'How are you feeling?' Cillian asks, plunking on to the bed by my feet.

Pulling my legs towards me to cross them, I look him in the eye. 'Uncomfortable.'

'That's to be expected.'

'Why did you lock me in here today?'

Cillian pulls down the corner of his mouth. He looks like a sad clown, only handsome. 'I didn't? If I did, I'm truly sorry. That really wasn't my intention.'

It's obvious he's lying by the way his cheeks turn a soft pink, and then he turns to scan the room as if looking for something. Evidence of a new escape attempt, probably. That bastard will do anything to keep me here. *Anything.*

That's what scares me.

'If it's any consolation, I have some good news for you.'

Naturally, I'm wishing for freedom. Anything else pales in comparison.

'What is it?' I dare to ask.

'We can take off your cast tomorrow.'

'It's been a week already?' I sit up. 'No way!'

'Way,' he says with a wry smirk. 'And you've been coming along nicely. Even had a good time of it, some might say. Look at all the care you've received. Most people would have to pay a fortune for all of this. But for you, my love, it's free.'

I shrink back towards the pillows, but not enough to look suggestive.

'You can come downstairs now,' he says, taking another sweep of the room with his eyes. 'The only thing I ask is that you behave yourself. No looking for your phone, no argumentative comments, and certainly no rushing for the door. All I want is for you to stay here and feel more comfortable. Is that fair enough?'

I nod absent-mindedly, deep in thought. Why am I not excited to have my cast removed? Oh, because it doesn't matter what you look like when you're dead, which I probably will be soon enough. See, I've known men like Cillian. It only starts with a pulling of the hair, and then it becomes a punch. Soon after that, it's blood and carnage.

'Thank you,' I say as sincerely as possible.

Cillian softens and gets to his feet, then waves me towards the door as if he hasn't done anything wrong this entire time. 'Come on,' he says excitedly. 'I'm going to make you some food and then allow you to have one small glass of wine for our cosy night in.'

With that, he's gone. Eerie silence fills the room. I know what most men think about when 'cosy nights in' become a possibility. I tell myself to remain calm and get ready to speak up against anything I don't want to happen. There are boundaries even Cillian shouldn't cross.

But it feels like he wants to.

Chapter 12
Daisy, Now

THE NEXT MORNING, Cillian promises to remove my cast somewhere around lunchtime. It's not clear why he's making me wait a few more hours, but I'm dying to get this horrible thing off my face and finally breathe out of my nose again. It's not that it's painful – it's just sort of suffocating, and I'm dying to get my head wet in the shower.

Interesting use of words in this house, that.

Dying.

Downstairs, there are bagels and a range of new cereals laid out on the dining table. There's a pitcher of milk and another one beside it filled with fresh orange juice. At first glance, it seems like Cillian is making a special effort for me, but then I hear a brand-new voice.

Spanish again. This time, male. Deep, kind.

There are flutters in my stomach as the voice draws nearer, his language a perfect rhythm. Cillian's voice replies to him, and that should cast a shadow over my hope, but it doesn't. I turn to see them both enter the dining room – Cillian and a dark-skinned man the same height as him. Stick-thin, strong-jawed, and kind-eyed. I smile as he comes in, to which he lazily raises a hand and grins toothlessly, spoiling that perfect picture.

But one thing lingers.

Hope.

'Comer,' Cillian says with a perfect accent, then gestures towards the dining table, where the man's eyes light up. 'Eat. Please. I'll be back in a few minutes.'

As he passes, Cillian plants a kiss on my head and leaves the room. I hope my shiver of disgust wasn't too obvious, but he's gone now. I'm alone in a room with someone who can help me – who can get me the hell out of here.

I give it a few seconds before heading for the door and making sure he's gone. Satisfied, I peer out of the window and see the work van sitting there. It's large and white with a small trailer attached to the rear. There's an image of a decayed, forgotten wasteland that slowly becomes a tropical paradise as you follow the horizontal line. Above it, a brand name:

MANUEL'S GARDEN SERVICES

'Your name is Manuel?' I ask, turning around.

By now, Manuel is already pouring one of the cereals into a bowl. He nods, still smiling, as he fills it with milk and then takes a seat at the table. His eyes are all over the food, even as he scoops cereal into his mouth, chews, and swallows.

'Garden service,' he says exotically.

'You work for Cillian?'

'Sí.'

I speed across the room, drag out a chair, and drop on to it. Our knees are touching, which clearly makes him uncomfortable, but it doesn't bother me in the slightest. 'Okay, listen,' I say, preparing to talk at the speed of light. 'Whatever Cillian told you, it's not true. I'm not his girlfriend, and I'm being held against my will. He talked me into staying here so he could help me recover from my surgery, but he won't let me leave. Please, you've got to help me. Call the police or fight him or... or *something*.'

Manuel swallows more cereal. Those beady eyes assess me. I'm waiting for something – anything – but every passing second drains the faith from my body. Then, in the fell swoop of just two words, he leaves me completely and utterly devastated.

'No inglés.'

My body sags, my head with it. As a force of habit, I reach into my pocket, looking for a phone to use the translator, but of course, it's not there. Why would it be? Not a single thing has gone my way since I made the stupid mistake of coming here. And now that Cillian enters the room and sits beside Manuel with a bunch of paperwork, it's become abundantly clear that I'm not going to get help from any of... well, the help.

I'm not going anywhere.

———

There is one good thing coming out of today: my cast is coming off.

Cillian makes me shower, which weakens the plaster. It's the first time in a week that I've been allowed to get my face wet, and it feels so refreshingly divine that I've already decided I'll take another in a few minutes. That will be to wash my hair thoroughly and stand under the water for ages, but right now, Cillian wants me back.

I fully dress back into my clothes before even leaving the bathroom – I don't want him getting any ideas – then head downstairs without putting the compression garment back on. It feels weird not wearing it. As if I'm doing some harm to my results by not having my face strangled all day and night. It incites some kind of panic that's hard to shake off.

Downstairs, Cillian is sitting in the living room. The early afternoon sun is beaming through the glass wall, but it hasn't quite reached the table, where a chair is pulled out right next to my captor. He gestures at it with a sweeping hand.

'Sit down, darling.'

Shuddering at that word, I swallow and do as I'm told, then swing my legs around to face him. I never did like people getting too close – even at the opticians when they get up real close and personal. As a rule of thumb, if you can smell their breath, then they're too close.

'It's nice and soggy,' he says, pressing his fingers against it. 'Does it hurt?'

'Not really. It's just a little sore.'

'Did you try pulling at it yet?'

'I thought it would be best to leave it to a professional.'

'Good choice.'

There's an odd tugging sensation when he peels at the plaster. I hear something tear, and I hold my breath while tape comes away from skin. Seconds later, the plaster cracks, and it peels off my nose. The sudden rush of air hits me. It feels like a weight has been lifted off my face. For the first time in a week, I can actually breathe. It's liberating.

'Remarkable,' he says, setting down the grim, disgusting cast and studying my new nose. 'You have no bruising whatsoever. Do you realise how lucky you are?'

Yes, so lucky, I think sarcastically.

Taking my cast off should be a good thing. I should be over the moon at finally being able to breathe. Cillian's beaming smile proves he's incredibly satisfied with the results, too, so what do I have to complain about? Oh, that's right.

Being a prisoner.

When I think about it hard enough, it's hard to get excited about my new appearance because it doesn't feel like anyone is even going to see it. At this point, I truly believe he won't let me go. That

I'll die up here in the middle of nowhere, whether that be forty years or forty days from now. The point is, I don't feel safe.

Cillian starts feeling around my face, telling me to look straight ahead. I obey for the most part, but every now and then, my eye catches his. I look away immediately, feeling so uncomfortable I'm just about ready to throw up.

'It's all looking good,' he says, sitting back and studying me with pride. Then he takes a hand mirror off the table that I didn't see until now and puts it into my hands. 'Are you ready to see your results?'

I should be intrigued by this, but I'm not. At least not until I raise the mirror and get a good look at the surgeon's work. That's when it hits me – a weird rush of pleasant surprise and gentle depression. I turn my head from side to side, marvelling at just how different I look. It looks great, almost completely changing the shape of my face. It's how I've always wanted to look, and without sounding egotistical, I finally look pretty.

'You're smiling,' Cillian says.

'I'm happy.'

'You should be.'

'Is this the final result?'

'No. It will change from month to month, but this is about sixty per cent of the result. You'll find the tip will drop, and the swelling will take a while to go down, but you're over the hardest part. Continue to sleep elevated on your back, and you should definitely take it easy for a few more weeks, which means it would be best for you to stay a little longer.'

It shouldn't crush me like it does. I wasn't expecting him to let me go at all, much less today, but just hearing from his own lips that he's not ready for me to leave puts me in a depressive state. I feel like a prisoner, locked away from the rest of the world. It's killing me, making me want to burst into tears all the time.

But Cillian is smiling.

'You look so beautiful,' he says. 'My beautiful angel.'

'Thank you...'

'I could kiss that face.'

There's an awkward pause. I rush to fill it.

'Can I shower as much as I like now?'

'Yes, you're probably dying to get your head wet. Go and enjoy a real shower for once. Do whatever you would normally do, but try not to get any chemicals on your nose for a couple more weeks.

Perhaps just give it one wash and then practise letting shampoo trickle down your back instead of your front.'

I nod. 'Thank you.'

'And you can start wearing the mask only at night now.'

'That's great news.'

Getting up and walking away, I should feel ecstatic about the way I look now. Between my nose, ears, and chin, there's such a significant improvement. The old Daisy isn't even recognisable in this new face, which should fill me with confidence. But I think knowing that nobody will ever see me makes it hard to get excited about.

I don't look back as I head for the stairs. All I can think about is how Cillian wanted to kiss me. There's no telling how long before he dares to actually try such a thing, and I don't want to be around when he suddenly gets the urge.

Because something tells me he won't take no for an answer.

———

At least the shower is everything I want it to be (and more).

Following Cillian's advice, I gently lather my nose with shower gel and get all the plaster residue off, then use a flannel to scrub the rest of my face. I wash my hair next – thoroughly – and the hot water over my head feels like heaven. I can practically feel a week's worth of sweat and dirt rushing through my hair and down into the plughole.

As soon as I'm done, I take a quick peek out the door, realise Cillian isn't there to perve on me, then hurry back to the bedroom with just the towel wrapped around me. I get my clothes on pretty quickly after that – washed and freshly pressed by the maid I haven't seen in a little while – and feel like a completely new woman. I can't stop looking at my results in the mirror. If only Lily could see this now. If only Jason...

No. I won't allow myself to think about him. I can't.

I think about something else. My escape. Manuel may not be very good at English, but if we spent a little time together, there's probably a way to communicate that I need help. It just means Cillian needs to leave us alone for a while... uninterrupted.

Wondering how to make this happen, I go to the window and see his van is no longer there. I didn't see him leave, and who even knows if he'll be back? The garden looks beautiful – too much for one man, really – but how much more work can really be done out there except for the maintenance? That does give me a little hope that he'll return.

He has to, because I can't stay here.

I slump on to the bed and fold my arms across my body. I keep seeing Cillian's expectant face as he mentioned that he wanted to kiss me. It's going to happen soon, and I can't think of anything worse. Well, I can, but *that* is a direct consequence of the kiss itself. Allowing myself down that lane of thought only makes me panic, my chest tight and my breath short.

I need to get out of here as soon as possible, I tell myself.

Before it's too late.

Chapter 13
Daisy, Then

ONCE AGAIN, I found myself in a taxi without the faintest clue as to where I was going. At this stage, I was starting to wonder if I was addicted to the drama of it all – the high-stakes thrill of being chased across the country and only narrowly escaping the man who came to get me.

The journey took almost an hour, stopping by some villages here or there before I told the driver to move on. Nowhere felt far enough away. It felt like wherever I went, I would always be found. I started to question how he was doing this – how he always seemed to know exactly where I'd gone and how to find me.

It took thirty minutes before I realised.

It was the credit card.

You saw it in films all the time: people would go on the run with the cops or FBI chasing them, and the very first thing they'd do was go off the grid. No phones, no credit cards. Nothing to trace them whatsoever. There was no way he was tracking my phone (at least, I didn't think so), but my credit card details were right there on my laptop. Did he think to look into that? It wouldn't have been that hard to figure out the last thing I'd paid for.

But how was I supposed to survive without money? If I went into a bank and suddenly withdrew a large amount of cash, there were certain things I could get away with, like paying for hotels or meals. But there was potentially at least one very large expense in my near future, and it was unlikely they'd take anything other than card.

I instructed the taxi driver to stop in a small town with one bank. He waited for me while I went inside. I withdrew what I needed and then got back in the taxi, barking at him to get me far away from there as if I'd just robbed the bank. That feeling of excitement came back again.

As did the cold, crippling fear.

Although the taxi driver wanted a conversation, I asked him to be quiet and let me think in peace for a while. He moodily turned on the radio, and then I watched the world go by and wondered where I was going to end up. The world had never felt so big and so small at the same time. I was finally free of Jason and could go anywhere in the country...

But for how long?

How long before I would be found again?

It was impossible to relax. My mind rebelled, thinking of as many things as possible in a desperate bid to keep me from formulating a plan. All that came up were the same problems: where to sleep tonight, where to get plastic surgery, and how I was going to get caught.

I'd never felt so stressed in my entire life.

And I suppose I deserved it.

ANOTHER DAY, another town, and *he* was far behind me.

Which paved the way for better things.

I was never really into drinking – my mother's problems with alcohol abuse had sent me in the opposite direction – but the past was catching up to me a little too fast. I desperately needed to relax, to have fun, even if it was by myself and just for a couple of hours.

The bar was right next to the hotel where I was staying. It was a low-ceiling kind of place with mellow music played by the handsome pianist in the far corner. The lighting was dim and kind on the retinas, the songs soft and relaxing. The barman wore a gorgeous black shirt under a silky-looking waistcoat, and he held himself properly while serving me and the only other customers: a married couple who spoke far too loud about their woes.

At least it was entertaining.

Right up until they left.

I nursed my vodka and lemonade, only slightly inebriated by the three or four drinks I'd consumed. My phone was in my pocket, but I was becoming too scared to turn it on. I was no Jason Bourne – I wouldn't have known how to fend off my attacker if he found me. Instead, I just sat there and let the gentle tones of the piano music wash away my worries, sinking into a pit of deep thought about the future and where it might take me.

I didn't even notice the music stop.

'Can I buy you a drink?'

The man's voice was strong and confident, but

for some reason, it didn't alarm me. Casually rotating my bar stool, I turned to find the pianist standing beside me. He was even more handsome up close, his good head of hair perfectly framing his masculine face. He had kind eyes and nice hands. A pianist's hands, of course.

'Only if you stick around to make sure I drink it,' I said.

'You have yourself a deal. The name's Chester.'

'*Chester?*' I asked, almost rudely.

Thankfully, Chester softly smiled as if he'd had this reaction a thousand times. 'I know, it's the worst name on earth. The kids gave me a hard enough time about it while I was growing up, so I decided to go by CJ. At least until I meet a beautiful woman and want to give her my real name, that is.'

'Are you... flirting with me?'

'Could be. How am I doing?'

'I'll let you know when I've drunk this.'

The barman put a drink down in front of me, right in time to point at it. I told Chester my name was Daisy and invited him to sit beside me. I was never used to having male attention, but Chester had a way of making me feel comfortable. The conversation flowed so naturally, and I genuinely enjoyed getting to know him. One drink turned into two, of course, which quickly turned into three or four more. The alcohol had started to get to me, which only made it easier to communicate with this beautiful man after his shift.

'What brings you out here?' he asked when he found out I was an out-of-towner.

'That's a long story,' I told him cryptically.

'Does this long story involve a man, by any chance?'

At this point, it was obvious he was fishing. He wanted to know more about me, which, given how I looked and how I felt about it, was kind of endearing. It was like he could see right through the ugly and into my soul. I wasn't proud of the things I'd done – particularly in recent history – but I did like to think I was a good person when you got right down to it. Perhaps that was why I warmed to this man so easily: he made me feel good again.

Unlike Jason.

It got me thinking...

'Listen,' I said, putting a hand on his. 'It sounds like a line, but I've never done this before. I'm from out of town, and it's a mystery as to where I'll end up next. The thing is, I like you, I think you like me, and—'

'Are you inviting me back to your hotel room?' he asked, cutting through the crap.

'What if I am?'

Chester stared right into my eyes. I stared back, my body tingling with excitement and fear and God knows what else. I waited forever for an answer, desperately wanting to be put out of my misery, even if it was destined to just be rejection.

Imagine my surprise when he leaned closer into my ear and said, 'One night only.'

'Fine by me.'

That was when he took my hand and led me out of the bar. I only pulled away to find the hotel room key in my bag, but even then, he kept stopping me to give the most intense and passionate kisses of my entire life. It felt awkward at first, as if I was cheating on Jason, but the more it happened, the easier it got. Needless to say, an hour later, I was lying on his sweat-glistened chest as our hearts beat in synchronised melody.

'I'm a very lucky man,' he said, panting. 'You're so beautiful.'

'I doubt it.'

'What makes you say that?'

I shrugged, dancing my fingers lightly across his chest. 'After a lifetime of being told you're ugly, you form an opinion of yourself. I don't like the way I look – never did – and no amount of kind compliments will make me believe otherwise.'

Chester's head tilted to look at me. 'You truly believe you're not stunning?'

'Correct.'

'Any way I can convince you?'

'Not really. I'm actually thinking about plastic surgery.'

'Wow. What kind of surgery?'

'Nose. Chin for sure. Maybe my ears, too.'

'Be careful. It can get addictive.'

'How do you know that?'

'My sister had some work done a couple of years ago. It started with a neck lift, but new things kept appearing on the list. Before she knew it, she was going in and out of surgery to make new changes. Between you and me, she looked better before all of that. That's not the surgeon's fault though – he was actually amazing.'

I tried listening to what he had to say, but I'd been so focused on fixing my flaws that there was no talking me out of it. 'This surgeon,' I said. 'Do you remember who it was?'

'Are you seriously asking for a recommendation from me?'

'Yes. Are you going to help a lady out?'

'Possibly. But first, let me try showing you how attractive I find you. If you still don't feel it afterwards, then ask me again, and I'll find you the surgeon's information. Deal?'

He didn't even wait for my agreement. I just smiled at Chester as he climbed back on top of me and expressed his excitement all over again. It wasn't as intense the second time – at least not for me – because all I could think about was that plastic surgeon.

And how badly I wanted his details.

***

CHESTER WAS GONE before the sun rose.

It didn't matter – I had everything I wanted: a night of passion with somebody who could give me validation, physical security until sunrise in case my past caught up to me, and the details of a plastic surgeon who was highly regarded.

No matter how wanted Chester had made me feel, however, my face still had to change. I'd been happy for a whole night, but if my happiness depended on the presence of a man, then I didn't want anything to do with it. It would just be another version of Jason, only under slightly different circumstances. I knew what I wanted, and I was going to get it.

I had the website open on my phone, lying on my back and scrolling through their before/after photos of the clients they'd operated on in the past. The results were impressive enough to warrant the high price tag, so it was just as well I had the money to pay for it.

There was just one problem. Paying for this surgery meant there would be a record of it on my bank statement. He would find me easily, only it would be much harder to run away from him as I'd be in the middle of my aftercare. I needed help, so I reached out to my cousin Lily just to ask if she wouldn't mind picking me up after a surgery. She had questions just like anyone else would, but she kindly agreed to do it.

It didn't matter where she dropped me off to, as long as it was far away.

I made the call that same morning, booking in a last-minute video consultation for the afternoon. We discussed all things surgical, from the procedure to the desired results, and then the lady on-screen covered what the aftercare would look like. I remember thinking it sounded like a lot of pain, but that it wouldn't be too difficult as long as Lily arrived to help me out.

We all make mistakes.

One thing was *not* a mistake though. This surgery was going to happen, and nobody was going to stop me. I'd wanted it all my life, but now I had the means *and* the motivation to finally go through with it all.

The truth wasn't exactly common knowledge, but *he* knew why I was doing this.

That was reason enough.

Chapter 14
Jason, Now

I spoke to Lily today, and the silly cow told me more than she should have.

Daisy was going to get some plastic surgery done, then get picked up from there. I acted like I knew what she was talking about, promised I'd do it instead, and then got all the details I would need. When she wasn't looking, I blocked Daisy's number on her phone.

Nothing would stand in the way of me getting to her.

Now, I'm sitting on the top of my Jeep with the sun beating down on my back. I don't own binoculars, so I use my phone camera to zoom in on the grand, isolated house in the distance. Apparently, this is where Daisy is staying, but I haven't seen a single trace of her.

It's a wonder I even got this information to begin with. The ladies at the surgery were very hesitant to give me even the slightest detail about their customer. A sort of confidentiality agreement must have been in place, but it didn't matter – a stranger in the local pub informed me she'd seen Daisy in the car with a man named Cillian.

Which brought me here.

It wasn't hard to find this man's address. The man – a Mr. Cillian White – owned a beautiful Aston Martin and the house I'm looking at now. There's no activity whatsoever, but I know Daisy is in there somewhere.

I hope nothing has happened to her.

Because I want to be the one to hurt her.

Chapter 15
Daisy, Now

OVER THE NEXT couple of days, Manuel comes and goes.

I'm trying to speak with him, but Cillian watches me like a hawk. Only yesterday, I told him I wanted to explore the surrounding countryside in peace to consider our future together. It worked for all of five seconds – a big grin plastered on his gaunt face – before he figured out what was going on. Not that he could prove it, but he suspected it enough to tell me no.

Today, I'm trying something different. I've noticed Manuel seems to arrive somewhere between eight and ten in the morning, so I'm up at six, complaining that I have a headache and need some air. Cillian is actually a sweetheart, rushing around to find me some paracetamol and apologising every time his voice creeps up in volume. When he puts the water down in front of me at the dining table, I gaze up at him pleadingly, faking a pained squint.

'I badly need some air,' I tell him.

'Okay. Let me find my shoes, and we'll—'

'Alone.'

Cillian stares down, but he's looking right through me. It's like he's trying to solve the world's hardest calculation, and the light behind his eyes dims for a moment. Then, when he suddenly returns to life, he shakes his head.

'That's not a good idea,' he says. 'What if you get weak and have a fall?'

'I'll go steady and stick to flat terrain.'

'What if it rains and you slip in the mud or something?'

'I'll take some wellies.'

'But you could easily—'

'Run away?'

The words are out of my mouth before I can stop them. Cillian's eyes become deadly slits that make me increasingly nervous with each passing second. I look away, unable to brave my way through this any longer. The truth is, he scares the ever-living hell out of me. There's no chance he's going to let me go. Not when there's a risk of me escaping.

Then...

'You can go out.'

My head snaps around to look at him now, my headache performance abandoned. My mouth hangs open, surprised as a thousand escape attempts flicker through my mind like some projector reel. Cillian starts to beam at me as if he's just given me the world.

If only he knew.

'You're welcome to walk around alone,' he goes on. 'As long as you stay within the grounds. I'll make sure the gate is locked just in case you get confused and start to wander. But yes, you're free to go and get some air out by the pool or something.'

'Alone?' I ask.

'Yes, alone.'

'Thank you.'

I'm doing my best not to laugh. Such good luck, so surprising in its timing. While Cillian heads outside to lock the main gate, I linger by the pool and let the chill morning breeze caress my neck. When he returns, I thank him and tell him how badly I needed this. Then he goes inside, and I pace back and forth along the impressive grounds, killing time by studying the rows of flowers and bushes that Manuel will soon be here to water.

What will I even say to him? His English isn't exactly great – even Cillian speaks to him in Spanish – but I could leave a note on the seat of his car. I think anyone with half a brain would look at a note in a foreign language and then use an online translator. Especially if the note uses one of the only Spanish words I actually know: policía.

But the morning goes on, and there's no sign of him.

Another couple of hours, and nothing.

By the time midday hits and the sun is harsh against my exposed skin, Cillian comes out to find me. There's only so long I can get away with this before my plan becomes obvious, so all there is to do is pray that Manuel comes soon.

Although he never does.

LATER THAT SAME DAY, I'm sitting in the living room with Cillian. The enormous TV is on. Some low-budget show set in a hospital is playing, and he watches in dead silence with his face scrunched up tight. It's obvious what he's doing: picking out the medical inaccuracies. It makes me wonder how much a plastic surgeon knows about general medicine.

Manuel still hasn't arrived, which does leave a question hanging in the air.

How much longer do I have to stay before someone can help?

I time my question well after a sneeze, which I have to do through my mouth as otherwise it could disrupt my nose's healing. I run to the bathroom to clean up what ended up in my palm, swill my mouth out with tap water, then return and mention the cause.

'Hay fever,' I mumble, rubbing my eyes and sitting back down.

''Tis the season,' Cillian says, still gawking at the TV.

'A lot of flowers on your property. Will Manuel be planting more?'

'Manuel is never coming back.'

The news hits me like a shovel swung right at my skull. Every ounce of hope floods from my body, my mood taking a sudden, severe dive. I have a thousand questions but no idea how to frame them. All I can do is try to hide my shock and make it look like casual conversation.

'Oh? How come?'

'There's not much more he can do.'

'What about watering the flowers?'

'It's not exactly a big job. I can do that myself.'

'Fair enough.'

I'll forever hate myself for leaving the conversation right there. It's impossible to pick back up again because all there is to say has already been said. Now, I'm sitting here just like before, completely hopeless and feeling like a prisoner all over again. My dreams of getting out of here and fleeing across the country are all but squashed.

Until Cillian's phone makes a noise.

I glance over as he scoops it up to read a text message. Then he gets up, hurries to the front door, and trudges down the gravel to open the front gate. I watch from the kitchen window, excitement replenishing in me so fast I'm just about ready to explode.

The gate is open, and the small car comes in. I've seen it before, so why wouldn't I be so happy I could throw up? The driver brings the car to a stop right outside the house while Cillian closes the gate once more. I clap a hand to my mouth just to hold in an ecstatic gasp. My prayers have been answered. Getting out of here suddenly seems possible all over again.

Because the maid has returned.

I MAY NOT GET to it right away, but I'm working on it.

It takes a whole day to get close enough to the maid. Her name is Isabella, and she's a lot prettier up close than I ever would have suspected from the distance of my bedroom window. The grey wisps of hair that caught in the sun no longer look like cobwebs, and what I previously thought of as chubbiness actually turns out to be a short and dumpy aesthetic that makes her look cutely compressed. It combines well with her merry behaviour, and – although she doesn't speak much English – she says everything she needs to say with a smile.

I wonder if she's worked out that it was me talking to her through the door.

Initially, I spent a day letting her warm to me. This is because it's likely Cillian was watching, and it was vital I made him think he could trust me. He thinks I didn't notice him pop his head around the door to check in on us, or sometimes his shadow would give away that he's standing outside the door and listening. This got less and less until the next day, when he finally left us alone long enough for me to say anything.

That time has come.

I see Isabella from across the room, minding her own business as she picks up the ornaments from the mantelpiece and dusts underneath them with the swift wipe of a pink rag. She's humming happily, in her own little world. It strikes me then that she's blissfully unaware of just how dangerous her boss is. Is he a danger to *her*, I wonder?

We'll find out when we get out of here.

'Isabella,' I say, passing by the window and seeing Cillian out front cleaning the pool. As soon as he has his back turned, I cross the room, take her hand, and lead her out of view. She's frowning as I pull her a little too forcefully, stopping her by the front door.

That's when she yanks her hand back and rubs her wrist, eyeing me suspiciously.

'Is hurt,' she says.

That's enough to get me excited – just two words of English. That can't be all.

'You need to help me,' I say loudly and slowly,

pointing at the both of us as if to punctuate each word. 'Cillian is a bad man. Do you understand? You need to leave, call the police, and send them up here.'

'Cillian,' she says, sounding a little dumb.

'Yes, Cillian.'

'Bad?' She points through the front door in his direction.

'Yes, bad. *Very* bad.'

'Why Cillian bad?'

'He's keeping me here. Erm...' I grasp the front door handle and pretend to try pulling it open, imitating a locked door and a trapped woman, then point at myself. 'Me – Daisy – no want inside. Daisy, please leave. Understand?'

Isabella's face is scrunched up tight while she strains to understand.

'Daisy... you?' she says slowly. Hesitantly.

'Yes. Me Daisy. Stuck. Cillian bad.' It feels like I'm talking to Tarzan. I might as well be. I come away from the door and hold her hand, staring into her eyes and knowing she's my last hope to get out of here alive. 'Please help.'

A silence fills the entrance then. My heart is racing. I want to scream at her to go get help, but she needs to figure this out, and no amount of pressuring is going to help her. This is something she has to reach on her own.

'Isabella... telephone?' she says, using her hand to gesture a phone. 'Nine-nine-nine.'

'Yes!' I almost scream at her, excitement flooding my veins. 'Nine-nine-nine. Emergency. Please, be quiet until you leave, and then tell the police to come here. You got it? Phone emergency. Police help Daisy. Cillian very bad—'

That's all I can get out before the front door makes a clicking sound and shoots open. Cillian appears so quickly that Isabella jumps back. Cillian freezes, watching her reaction. There's no way in hell he hasn't figured out what's been happening. And if that wasn't enough, she takes a giant step back as he comes inside, mumbles something in Spanish, then disappears into the next room as though she's forgotten something.

'Is something wrong?' he asks me.

As naturally as possible, I shake my head. 'Why would there be?'

'Because of that.' Cillian nods towards where she left the room.

'She's acting a little weird. I think she's scared of me.'

'Huh. Looked more like she was scared of *me*.'

'Why would she be scared of you?'

'That, my love, is a good question.'

Cillian closes the door, locks it. Takes out the key. Then he tucks it into his pocket and kisses me on the cheek. It takes everything I've got not to cringe as he does this, but somehow, I manage to force a soft, convincing smile.

'Promise me,' he whispers in my ear, letting me feel his size up against me – reminding me how much bigger, stronger, and faster than me he really is. 'Promise me you weren't trying anything funny. It would be a shame for something to happen to you after all we've gone through. After all the work we've done on your perfect face.'

I swallow. Hard. I try finding the words – any words at all – but nothing comes out of my mouth as I already feel suffocated. All I can do then is nod, make a sound of easy agreement, then try not to cry as he walks past me and into the kitchen. It's hard to say if help is coming.

I'm not sure Isabella understands.

Chapter 16
Daisy, Now

THIS FEELS like the wait of my life.

Not only has it been a long, sleepless night waiting for Isabella to return, but I awake in the morning to find she still hasn't showed up. For some reason I'll never understand, I'm still expecting police sirens to come wailing down the road. What would happen if they did, anyway? Would Cillian react aggressively or concede peacefully on his knees?

There's only one way to find out.

As if I'll ever get that chance.

Morning comes, the sun cresting over the horizon in harsh oranges that sting my tired eyes. I can barely keep them open, fatigue tugging at the lids like they're daring me to sleep. I don't want to.

Not if there's even the slightest chance of missing the police.

But are they even coming?

Isabella didn't say bye yesterday, and I wonder if she got home okay. My exhausted imagination is conjuring up all sorts of thoughts: she veered off the road in a desperate hurry, or the police didn't hear her. Perhaps she simply didn't understand what I was trying to tell her.

In that case, I'll have to try again when she returns.

And again.

And again.

At least Cillian seems to have believed nothing was wrong. We pass each other in the kitchen first thing, but he only smiles and wishes me good morning before disappearing into his study for the next few hours. It crosses my mind that I could run now, but how far would I make it? It's miles back to town, and even if I made it, what then?

How much could I prove?

I decide it's best to calmly endure the wait. It gets to lunchtime, and Cillian appears, asking if I would like a sandwich. Actually, I'm starving, so I perch on a kitchen stool and suck up to him while he butters bread and slaps around slices of honey roast ham.

'It is commendable,' I say, watching him prepare lunch, 'that you have all this money, all this help, but still choose to do the simple chores yourself. Like making lunch, for example. Which I would have done for us, I might add.'

'Thanks.' Cillian presses down the top slice of bread, compressing the sandwich and then sliding the plate in my direction before leaning on his hands. 'But you should be resting. Like I said, you're a guest, and it would be inappropriate to have you prepare the food.'

You mean you don't trust me, I think. *Because I'm tempted to poison you.*

The sandwich is great – soft bread, thick ham, and a healthy dose of rocket salad to balance the flavour. There's no sauce, which works for me. The problem is, I can't eat it too fast for fear of not being able to keep it down. I'm too damn anxious.

'No Isabella today?' I ask, passing it off calmly after a big swallow.

'Not likely, no.'

'Oh, how come?'

'I had to let her go.'

I'm two milliseconds away from hurling, the

news taking me by surprise like a chokehold. It's impossible to keep the shock out of my eyes, despite how hard I try.

'Why?' The word comes out too blunt, so I add, 'Is she not doing a good job?'

'That's my business.' Cillian winks, but there's no smile.

'But I thought she was doing just fine. Were you not happy with her?'

'Let's just say she's a snoop.'

'So she's *never* coming back?'

'Certainly not. Why?'

I shake my head like I don't have an answer. Which I don't. Even as he stares at me, challenging me to tell him the truth that I'm pretty convinced he already knows, I just can't bring myself to sit up straight and tell him it's time for me to leave.

Hell, it was time a few days ago.

I never should have come here.

Cillian huffs disapprovingly, turns, then throws his sandwich in the bin. I watch, stunned, as he has his little outburst and then storms out of the room. I want to ask him what's wrong just to break the awkwardness, but we both know what's wrong.

He's figured out I was asking for help, and he doesn't like it.

Not. One. Bit.

———

An hour later, when the sandwich is gone and I've been trying to relax with my feet up on the sofa, Cillian appears in the doorway with a thunderous look on his face. Needless to say, it's very unsettling, but I try to act like everything is okay.

'Can we talk?' he asks.

'Absolutely.'

I'm not sure what to expect when he comes inside slowly, takes a seat in front of my bare feet, then takes a deep breath. Maybe an apology just like last time, and maybe – just because I like to punish myself with foolish hopes – a promise to let me go.

Then he blows it all over in one fell swoop.

'You should go upstairs to your room.'

That lingers in the air like a bad smell. I'm speechless, partly wanting to ask if I've done something wrong but mostly thinking it's best to just do what he says and not argue. What is it they say – don't poke the bear?

'It's nothing personal,' he says, placing a hand on my knee. 'It's just that there's something I must do, and I don't entirely trust you enough to keep out of the way. I can make you go up there by force, but isn't it nicer that I asked?'

There's something in his eyes that I don't like, as well as a thousand questions knocking around in my head about what he's up to and why he doesn't want me to see. This much is clear: the worst thing I could do right now is ask him. The second-worst thing is to disobey.

Without another word, I'm on my feet and heading up the stairs. Cillian follows closely, not saying anything as I march my way back to what I often misconstrue as a prison cell. When I'm inside, he turns the key in the lock and leaves me in the dead silence.

What the hell?

The weirdness doesn't end there. As the minutes slowly roll by, I can't help but think he's up to something sinister. My mind is wandering, conjuring up a million different things he might be doing. None of them good. All of them deadly. It gets me thinking of Isabella and how lucky she is to have been let go. There are worse ways to leave this house.

That's what I fear the most.

I don't feel like watching TV, and my brain is far too busy to allow reading, so I sit on the windowsill with every intention of watching the birds flock over the horizon. Maybe even try forming images from the different shapes in the clouds. But none of that happens.

Because of what I see below.

It's hard to believe at first. I question whether I misheard Cillian because the car sitting by the front door most definitely belongs to Isabella. Has she come back, or did she never really leave in the first place? Was he lying to me, or did I simply get the wrong end of the stick? The only thing I can think of is that she's come back to collect some things. Perhaps that's why I'm locked in here – so I can't make one last, desperate bid to communicate with her.

Sadly, none of that turns out to be true.

From this angle, all I can see is an arm. A man's arm. Cillian's. It reaches out for the car boot, raising the door before he leans in and clears some space. I shoot to my feet and press my cheek against the glass, hoping to get a better view. By the time I'm in a position to see anything, Cillian has exited the car and gone out of sight.

He returns moments later with three large black bags.

I'm no idiot – I'm fully aware of the theory presenting itself in my mind. Cillian's behaviour towards me may well be the driving force behind my conclusion, but it's certainly a plausible theory. I watch him now, sweat forming on my brow as he struggles to heave the three bags into the back of Isabella's car. Then, watching while my mind and heart race in synchronisation, Cillian gets in the car and drives it through the gate, closing it behind him before heading far into the distance until he becomes little more than a greenish dot.

Baffled and petrified, I step away from the window and start biting my nails. It's hard to keep my trembling fingers still. All I can think about is the shape of those bags – the obvious weight as Cillian struggled to place them in the back. Why did he drive away in her car? Where was she? Deep down, I think I know.

I'm just too scared to accept the truth.

AFTER A FEW MINUTES of stunned silence, another thought pollutes my head.

What if Isabella is still alive and needs my help?

There has to be a way out of here, and I don't care what it will take to explore the house. The logical, rational part of my brain knows there are only two ways to leave this room: the door or the window. The door is not an option, which quickly has me opening the window and leaning out. As luck would have it, the adjacent window is also open. My gaze travels down to the ledge between the two. It's thin, *might* hold my weight, but there's no guarantee.

Nonetheless, I have to try.

Praying Cillian doesn't return while I cling to the side of the house for dear life, I put one foot out on the ledge to test its strength. Even when I kick it hard with my heel, not so much as a single stone crumbles from the ledge. Breathing heavily, I put both feet out and slowly lower my weight on to it. I expect it to collapse at any moment.

It never does.

The gutter is all I can hold on to, but it doesn't need much clinging on to. Just a soft touch to maintain my balance while I shimmy along the ledge. It takes all I have not to look down as I go, inching closer and closer to the next window, until...

I make it, practically falling through the window and landing on the floor with a thud. My elbows take the pain as I let out a delighted squeal of surprise. I'm on my feet in an instant, rushing for the door to find it's not only unlocked but open. Somehow, using nothing but dumb hope and a ton of desperation, I've made it safely out of my room.

Just not out of the house.

I try the front door, of course, but to no avail. It's locked, and the key is gone. Why wouldn't it be? Cillian is a smart man who would do anything to keep me here, so it doesn't surprise me that he has every angle covered. What he didn't account for was the long glass wall in the living room. I rush in there and grab a hideous china replica of the Eiffel Tower, ready to hurl it through the glass and grant myself freedom.

Then I see it.

It's not the bright pink fabric that grabs my attention. Nor is it the white frills. But the splotches of scarlet on the collar and cuffs scream for my attention. I lower the ornament. It slips from my hand and lands on the rug. My heart in my throat, I approach Isabella's blouse and sink to my knees. A small, weak, guttural sound escapes my mouth.

I've seen enough TV shows to know that I shouldn't touch it. Prints and fibres – all of that CSI stuff that could easily be used against me. But I'm close enough to know the blouse belongs to Isabella, and that's definitely blood. *Her* blood.

My frantic brain rushes to piece everything together: the car, the black bags and the visible weight of them, and now this. No matter how much I try to deny it – even as I vaguely make out Cillian walking through the field in the distance and know I need to get back to the room – Isabella has been killed by my captor. Her body is stashed in that car.

And I could easily be next.

Chapter 17
Daisy, Then

I'VE BEEN LYING to you. It's only a little lie.

Ah, who am I kidding?

This is the biggest lie in history.

I should tell you the story again, but truthfully this time.

When I told you I got up and left Jason in the middle of the night, that was only partly true. I really *did* leave him, and it really was in the middle of the night, but there were bits in between that really deserve our attention, if you'll indulge me.

See, he came back from the pub long before I got to sleep. I'd been lying in bed, a book spread open across my chest that I couldn't settle my mind enough to read. All I could think about was that this cycle was just going to repeat itself over and over. I would cook, clean, get bullied for it, then carry on pretending everything would change someday.

But it never would.

When I'm stressed, I tend to bake, so I threw the covers off me, went downstairs, and began to prepare the ingredients for a basic Victoria sponge cake. My heart wasn't really in it, but at least I wasn't hiding between the sheets and suffocating myself with thoughts of where my life was going – how bad things had become.

I wasn't far into it, barely getting everything together in a neat row as I always liked to do, when the front door opened and a burst of cold air crept in. My heart sank immediately, fear instantly taking control of my body and giving me the shakes. I didn't bother looking at him because I could smell the alcohol, and no good could come from interacting.

'Not even going to say hello to your own fella?' he slurred lazily.

If only to satisfy him, I turned and leaned against the kitchen counter, looking him up and down. He was in a real bad state – could barely stand up straight without starting to wobble. The dizziness must have been kicking in, and experience told me that was when he was at his worst. In these situations, it was always better to placate him.

'Did you have a nice time?' I asked.

'Don't act like you give a shit.'

'But I do.'

'Heh.' Jason chuckled, wobbled, and held on to a kitchen chair for stability. 'Treating me like an idiot. You *always* treat me like such a bloody idiot.'

'That's not true. I—'

'Don't interrupt me!'

I shrank back against the counter. By now, his wandering gaze couldn't even find me. I found myself growing angrier and angrier at the repetition of this ongoing behaviour, but that was something we could deal with later. Right now, he needed to go to bed.

Doing my best to help him, I stepped forward and put a hand against his chest. Out of nowhere, he clamped a hand over my shoulder like a vice, then gave me the hardest shove I'd ever experienced in my entire life. I stumbled backwards, hit the counter once more, then stood up straight and gave in to the heat burning up through my chest.

'Will you stop bloody hurting me?' I screamed. *Shrieked.*

Then his eyes found me, and I knew from his dark stare that I'd crossed the line. He was on me in an instant, first slapping me with a horrendous thunderclap sound that made my head swim, then a punch that knocked the wind out of my stomach. I gasped for breath, wheezing so badly it sounded like a squeak. Then, he used all of his drunken strength to push me.

I reached out for something to hold on to, but it was too late. A bunch of items made their way from the counter to the floor: the mixing bowl, an unopened bag of flour, and a bunch of bills that were still waiting to be paid. There were other things, too.

But I hadn't seen them yet.

Jason stood over me like a dark tower of pain and misery. His teeth were gritted, his fists shaking like he just couldn't keep the anger down any more. I would leave him, I decided then – if I somehow survived tonight, I never wanted to see him again.

'Think you're so perfect, don't you?' he spat. 'Like nothing you do is wrong.'

Still wheezing, I rolled on to my front and tried to crawl away. But I couldn't breathe – could hardly see straight through the explosion of pain and the fear. The same fear that had killed the sweet, vibrant young woman I'd once been.

'You don't honestly think you can get away from me, do you?'

Truthfully, I didn't, and that was the most terrifying part of it all. Jason was a big man. A *cruel* man. It was time to leave him, but first, I would have to survive the night. I found anger coursing through my veins like hot lava, feeling true hate for the first time in my life. They say that if you repeatedly back a harmless dog into a corner, someday, it will no longer be harmless. I felt like that dog now because I badly wanted to hurt Jason.

That was when I crawled forward ever so slightly and found it.

On the floor, right in front of me, was a knife.

———

Jason's laugh was cruel and taunting. It was like he knew I didn't have the strength to fight him or the courage to even stand. Perhaps that was what made me try so hard – spurring me on to fight my way to my knees, gripping the kitchen counter with one hand as a means to clamber to my feet. My other hand was being used already.

It was the one gripping the knife.

I turned to face him, taking one big step back. My breathing was slowly getting easier, but it sort of rattled through my breath, laboured. I held the knife out in front of me, the shiny stainless steel shaking as badly as the hand that held it. At this point, I was pretty convinced I'd never have the balls to do it.

That would soon turn out to be terribly wrong.

'Are you going to kill me?' Jason asked, knocking his head back to laugh. He was hunched over, swaying, but still had inches on me. It was a part of what made him so terrifying – the sheer size of him. 'I reckon you should quit messing around and do it.'

'Leave me alone!' I yelled.

'Aww, don't be like that,' he mocked, opening a shirt button and tapping at his massive chest. 'Come on, I'll even give you an opening. Just stab me right here, sweetheart. Or is that yet another thing you can't do right?'

I wanted to – God knows I wanted to – but how could I justify murder? Even with somebody as horrible as Jason, there had to be a way out. A way that didn't involve trying to kill him. It was only then that I realised the true reason he wasn't already dead.

It wasn't because I was scared to kill him.

It was because I was scared I *could.*

This version of me was something I hated with a passion. Perhaps even more than I hated Jason, which was saying something. He was still standing there with his shirt open, mocking and taunting me while the knife continued to tremble in my sweaty grip. I wanted it so badly – to end his life and claim just that last fraction of power for myself.

'That's what I thought,' he spat. 'A coward as well as a bitch.'

'Stop calling me that.'

'What? A bitch? You *are* a bitch, Daisy. Everyone knows it.'

'Shut up, you bloody arsehole!'

As soon as those words uncontrollably left my lips, his eyes widened. The air grew hotter. Jason stomped forward, the weight on his shoes slapping against the kitchen floor tiles. I backed away, my spine slamming into the freezer that hummed merrily, like ignorance was bliss. By then, Jason was right in my face, his sour, stinking breath making me turn my head to one side as he wrapped his hand around my throat and started to squeeze.

'You made a mistake by threatening me,' he hissed. 'Let me remind you who's in charge here. *I'm* the man, and you're the worthless little wench that needs to take care of the house. When are you going to get that through your stupid head, you dumb bitch?'

My primal instincts took over then. That word worked as a trigger for me. I was still holding the knife, I realised, but my mind was working a damn sight slower than my body. I felt the plunge of the steel tip before I even knew I'd done it. Jason's eyes shot open, sobering him. A weak, pathetic breath breezed through my lips.

Jason stepped back, taking the knife in his stomach with him. Confused, as if the pain was yet to hit him, he looked all around the room before looking down and seeing it. It's hard to explain what happened next, but I experienced a sharp, sudden fear that he was going to survive it – that he would grow even angrier and punish me for my rebellion.

There was only one thing to do.

I rushed forward and pulled it out. Jason bellowed a word I didn't understand, then swung for me and missed. It was too late for him now, as I shoved the knife back into him, three inches from the previous wound. Then, suddenly, all the hate I'd ever felt for him boiled to the surface. I found myself pulling the knife out and stabbing it back in. Pull, stab, pull, stab. It went on like that until he sunk to the floor, crying like a little boy who so badly wanted his mother.

Before I knew it, I was on the floor with him. I dropped the knife, which clattered to the floor. My arms found their way around him, and I held my husband, bawling my eyes out, while he slowly died a quiet, undignified death.

I wasn't sure what had really happened tonight, but I knew one thing for certain.

Jason was dead.

And I was a killer.

A THOUSAND THOUGHTS rush through your mind after murder.

Why did you do that?

What happens now?

Where will I put the body?

Life would be different now – that much was true – but just how different could it really get? Jason would no longer be there to bully me and make me feel small. In fact, as I sat on the floor with his lifeless body in my arms, it became immediately clear that there would never be a need to feel small again. There was nobody left to bully me.

He was gone, and he wasn't coming back.

But this was his house, and people would come knocking. What would I tell them? That he'd gone away for a trip and never returned? There was no way I could keep up a lie like that – the police would soon come knocking, and I would definitely give in quickly.

All the same, I couldn't resist just sitting there.

I caressed Jason's head as it lay in my lap, stroking his hair as though he could feel it. Those wide, angry eyes stared up at me, piercing me with that fierce gaze. The whole time, I tried thinking about something as nearby as tomorrow. What would my first day alone look like? Was it possible to just wake up, eat breakfast, and carry on as normal?

No, it was best I got as far away from there as possible.

Anyway, I still felt ugly. Jason had seen to that. There was a strong chance of surgery in my future – whatever it took to alter my face – but that was probably later down the line. First, I had more urgent priorities. See my earlier question.

Where will I put the body?

It was time to get up and take care of business. This kitchen had to be cleaned from top to bottom, and Jason's body had to be removed. *Hidden.* The idea that he was dead hadn't quite sunk in yet, so I did my best to stay practical and focus on the fact that he was an object that needed burying. And fast.

It took all my strength to get up off that floor, but somehow, I managed. It was like my body was on autopilot, taking the controls while I blacked out from sheer panic. Before I knew it, the kitchen was clean and my husband's body in the back of our car.

My car, I corrected myself.

There would be a lot of that in my future, as we'd shared so much. To be honest, there would be a lot of times that I'd confuse names and places. The coming days were one of those examples because although I've acted like Jason was chasing me from town to town, it wasn't him after all. It couldn't have been because that man was dead.

And my real pursuer knew it.

Chapter 18
Daisy, Now

I HEAR THE FRONT DOOR, and I'm still unable to move.

It's threateningly loud, as are Cillian's feet when he stubs them against the mat. I'm still rooted to the spot, every fibre of my being telling me I have to run for my own survival, but the signal's just not reaching my body in time.

Cillian closes the front door, and only then do I manage to stand upright. I'm stunned by what I found – by Isabella's bloody blouse – and that's when it registers that if I'm not back in my room when Cillian comes to see me, I may suffer the same fate as her.

When I hear the footsteps, I slide out of the

room and rush for the stairs. The floorboards don't creak, but the soles of my shoes do hit the wood loud enough to panic. I freeze at the first sound, one hand on the banister as fear ricochets through me.

'Is someone there?' Cillian asks.

There's a pause as I close my eyes and curse under my breath. Then, when I hear movement from the next room, I hurry up the stairs towards my bedroom. Cillian follows, asking more questions and threatening a potential intruder with their life. It makes me wonder.

If he knew it was me, would he still be angry?

Of course he would. He's made no effort to hide his control over me. It's been in every move he's made. Every move *I've* made. Including now, running back to the room with a cold chill running through me like poisonous ice.

I reach the room, grab the handle. It doesn't budge. I curse again, remembering there's no easy way back inside. Then I rush to the adjacent room, knowing I can skip the whole process of testing my weight against the ledge, hurry along the wall, and slip inside.

Just as my feet touch the carpet, the door bursts

open. I let out a short gasp as Cillian swings inside, standing there and looking me up and down as though he knows exactly what I've been up to. It's like he's been watching the whole time.

'Where have you been?' he asks.

'Right here,' I lie. 'Why?'

'Then why are you out of breath?'

'Because you startled me.'

Cillian studies me, looks at the open window, then back at me. As if he thinks someone has sneaked inside his home and is taking refuge, he checks behind the door and under the bed. I don't move the entire time, except for closing the window quietly. When he's done, he returns to the door and holds the handle, filling up the doorway to keep me in.

'You're acting different,' he says.

'Am I?'

'Did you... see something?'

Like you loading the car with a dead body and driving it away? That's what I want to say, but instead, I just shake my head and try not to make a show of swallowing whatever dry lump has been forming in my throat. Somehow, I also hide my shakes.

AJ Carter

'Why aren't you asking more questions?' he says.

'What do you mean?'

'I've just rushed in here looking for someone and suspected you of seeing something. Anyone who's completely innocent would wonder why I've done any of that, but you haven't asked so much as a single question. What are you hiding?'

It's not easy, but I somehow manage a nonchalant shrug. 'Maybe I was just raised differently. It's none of my business what you do in your own home. Whatever you think I saw, I'm obviously curious about, but at the end of the day, it's not my place to ask questions.'

Cillian eyes me up and down again, like he's trying to figure out if my response is good enough. My body is so tense the entire time that I don't know if I might explode. I wait in the silence, not quite knowing where to look, until – finally – he speaks.

'If you did see something and you do want to know, just ask.'

'Yeah, okay.'

Taking one last long look at me, Cillian nods and leaves, shutting the door behind him. This time, he doesn't lock the door. I wonder if he knows he's left Isabella's blouse behind and that I could easily find it if I simply go downstairs without waiting for him to find it – to find and hide it like it's going to make a difference.

Like I don't already know the truth.

HOURS GO BY, during which I spend a lot of time downstairs because I want to act as relaxed as possible. I believe it's vital to my survival, not letting him know just how petrified I really am. The more time that goes by, the more convinced he seems that I'm innocent.

That I didn't find his dirty little secret.

We make it all the way to dinner time, when he asks me to wear a nice dress for dinner. I tell him I don't own a nice dress as I never expected to be staying in such good company – I deserve a goddamn Oscar for *that* performance – and then he says I should wear one anyway.

While he cooks downstairs, I shower (still enjoying that feeling since removing my cast) and slip into the dress. It's fine, it really is, but I feel dirty wearing it. As if I'll be eye candy in exchange for being here. Not that I want to be here any more.

Actually, I want the opposite.

When I'm all dressed up, I head downstairs and into the dining room. Cillian watches me enter as if I'm some kind of prom date. He blows out a breath and admires me. It feels like insects are crawling all over my skin. Goosebumps rise on my bare arms.

'You look incredible,' he says like he just can't believe it. 'You said it's not a nice dress.'

Is it weird that the compliment hits me in a very slightly pleasing way? That's what you get after a lifetime of being told how ugly you are – now I'm being told I'm beautiful by a man whose job is to study and perfect the shapes of faces.

It's not long before we're sitting down to dinner. Cillian doesn't bother to dress up, but he doesn't need to. He looks just fine in his flannel shirt, the sleeves rolled up and the top button exposing his hairy chest. He serves up a pasta dish, tomato and herb bread, and a pot of something I dare not touch because it reminds me too much of blood.

'Tuck in.'

I don't realise how hungry I am until the first

forkful is in my mouth. Then I can't seem to stop eating, shovelling the meal into my mouth as if I'll starve if it doesn't all get devoured in five minutes or less. The only thing that does manage to stop me is Cillian.

His choice of words alone is enough to scare the life out of even the bravest woman.

'Isabella told me more about you than I ever wished to learn.'

The fork falls from my hand and clangs against the china plate. 'What?'

'She told me you had a little conversation with her. About me.'

'I forgot you speak Spanish.'

'That's not the point.'

'Yeah...' I suck in a deep breath and prepare myself for what's coming, desperately trying to think of some way to cover myself. The problem is, I can't do that without knowing exactly what Isabella told him. 'What was said?'

'She said you wanted help.'

'What kind of help?'

'"Emergency."'

I clasp my hands together and rest my chin on my knuckles, staring at him from across the table. For a moment, it doesn't look like there's a way out of this. Isabella speaks – *spoke* – very good Spanish, but I quickly remember just how bad her English was.

'Is that what she said?' I ask.

'Do you deny it?'

'That depends on the context.'

'Enlighten me.'

'I wasn't going to tell you this...' Sitting back, I brush a hand through my hair and then grip the arms of the dining chair, looking across at him with as much courage as I can muster. 'But I spilled some blackcurrant juice on your rug. It looked really expensive, just like everything else in this house, so I asked her to clean it before the stain set in.'

Cillian eyes me suspiciously. 'And that was an emergency, was it?'

'Spanish is lost on me. I thought of the best words she'd understand.'

'You told her I was a bad man.'

'No, I told her you would *feel* bad if you found out about the rug.'

'And you didn't think to tell me this?'

'Thought I got away with it. Look, I'm really sorry.'

Slowly, deliberately, Cillian gets up and crosses

the room, dropping the needle on a gorgeous oak vinyl player. Paul Anka's voice sings gently through the speaker, just loud enough to enjoy without drowning out our voices. Then, Cillian returns to his seat and continues to eat his dinner. He only stops a minute later, when something occurs to him.

'Isabella didn't understand what you said,' he tells me.

'That's right.'

'Yet, there's still no stain on the rug.'

I'm trying so hard not to visibly sweat. 'Cleaned it myself.'

'If you say so. Anyway, I had to let her go. You won't be seeing her again.'

Because you killed her, I think, picking up my fork and trying to eat.

The rest of the meal is highly uncomfortable, sitting in silence with Cillian occasionally looking up at me. I've done something wrong – I know it, he knows it – and Isabella is the one who suffered from my mistake. How much longer must this go on, I wonder? When, if ever, will this dangerous man release me back into the wild?

Another song comes to its end, and one more starts. Cillian sits back and makes a sound of both surprise and pleasure, and then he's on his feet and coming to my end of the table with his hand extended and a weirdly excited smile forming dimples on his cheeks.

'I love this song,' he says. 'Dance with me.'

It's not like I have a choice any more, is it?

I NEVER WAS much of a dancer, and that wasn't going to change.

Still, Cillian has me on my feet and in his arms without me getting a say in the matter. His hands are on my hips, my arms slung around his neck. His cologne is pleasant, but nothing else is. Especially not the lingering threat of death.

'You look beautiful tonight,' he says.

'Thank you.'

'Do you think I look nice?'

'You look fine.'

I know a comment like that is likely to make him angry, but it's better than letting him think there's some kind of attraction between us. The comment rolls off him, and we continue to dance. Even having never heard the song before, I hate it. It feels like it's going on forever and ever. By the time it does finally come to an end, the vinyl has finished playing, and we're swaying in the silence. There's not an ounce of comfort in me the whole time.

'Do you think we're moving too slow?' he asks.

'What do you mean?'

'You've been here a while now, and we haven't even kissed.'

'To be fair, the circumstances are—'

It's hard to finish a sentence when a man's tongue is in your mouth. I instinctively pull back, pushing against his shoulders to get away from him. The taste lingers. A man's taste. I wipe my moist lips with my bare wrist and try not to show my disgust.

'Do I repulse you?' he asks, shame and regret resting on his features.

'No, it's not that. It's just...' I rummage around in my brain for any excuse. 'It's been a long time since anyone but my husband kissed me. I also feel a little sensitive after all the surgeries. It hurts... Even if I was comfortable with it, it physically hurts.'

Cillian holds my gaze, his eyes seeing right through me. He's deep in thought, trying to discern whether I'm lying. The science of his art supports my comment because he knows as well as I do that rhinoplasty and liposuction can be sore for weeks after surgery.

'Fine,' he says, then storms out of the room without another word.

Something tells me he feels anything but fine.

Chapter 19
Daisy, Now

ANOTHER DAY, another opportunity to accidentally upset my erratic captor.

Sometimes it's hard to believe I have one of those – a captor. Most people would kill to live in a house like this. Technically, I did do that, but I try not to let the memory of my ex-husband's demise fill my head. There's enough going on up there to keep me going for a lifetime. The less cluttered I can keep it, the better.

I haven't seen Cillian since he walked out on me during the dance. This is highly unusual, considering I've been hanging around downstairs as much as possible to try to catch his attention. The more an angry man ruminates on his pain, the harder it gets for him to deal with. The last thing I want to engage with is that.

At around two the next afternoon, when I'm bored of reading and dreaming of an outside world, I go for a wander around the house. I start just upstairs, where the windows allow a gorgeous view of the plains surrounding the house. It's stunning – the vibrant green grass, birds flocking together, a sun so bright it burns my retinas – but this is a dangerous game to play. I'm only making things worse for myself by thinking of a life I'll never actually get to live. Because, let's face it, I'm probably stuck here forever.

But it doesn't have to be that way.

Desperate to get away from the dream-inducing vistas, I head downstairs and begin to pace those hallways instead. I don't get very far before noticing Cillian's office door is open again, the sunlight pouring through and spilling on to the hallway carpet. Quietly, I approach the entryway and prepare to say hello to Cillian.

But he's not there.

It's a good thing. A *great* thing, because his computer is still on and completely unattended. Most people would seize an opportunity to go and use it – to finally make an escape somehow by reaching the outside world – but something is wrong. I can feel it. Cillian would never leave that opportunity for me unless it's a trick or if he intends to return in—

'Don't get any ideas.'

The voice comes from my right, and it doesn't surprise me in the slightest. I crane my neck to see him standing there in a smart grey business suit without the jacket, a cup of steaming coffee in one hand, and a sparkle of humour in his eyes.

'You look chirpy,' I tell him.

'Why wouldn't I be?'

'I just thought after yesterday...'

Cillian flaps a dismissive hand, goes inside to set down the mug, and sucks a drop of coffee off his thumb. A moment later, he's coming back out of the room and puts a hand softly on my shoulder as he leads me towards the stairs.

'Yesterday was yesterday,' he says, heading upstairs and encouraging me to follow, which I do without question. 'Today is a new day, and all new days need to be celebrated. I've got a beautiful home, an amazing job, and the woman of my dreams.'

'The woman of your dreams?'

'It's you, Daisy.'

'Of course.'

'And because of how much I care for you, I got you a little something.'

I dread to think what it might be, but I go with him to the top of the stairs and towards the far end of the hall. Cillian is growing more possessive, and it's starting to seriously unnerve me. But what can I do about it if I want to keep him calm?

'Nothing' is the answer. Like he said, I'm his.

Whether I like it or not.

ALTHOUGH AT FIRST IT looks as if we're going back to my bedroom, Cillian stops outside a room I've never been in before. Using a key he pulls from his pocket, he unlocks it and shoves open the door to let us both inside.

It's a mostly empty room that smells of something old, like it's been forgotten in time. Sunlight is bleeding through the window, the brightness illuminating the many dust motes that dance in the air. The floorboards creak beneath our weight, and there's nothing to look at save for a giant wardrobe at the back of the room. It lurks there in antique grandeur, and I'm already wishing it would take me all the way to Narnia.

Just to get away from him.

'I went shopping the other day,' he says, opening the double doors together and riffling through the hanging garment bags. 'There was a small pop-up market in town that sold elegant dresses but with poor craftsmanship. It got me thinking about how you didn't bring many clothes and how yesterday you said you didn't like your dress, so this morning, I took a trip and picked up something a little more... you.'

As he picks a covered dress off the rail and unzips it, I can't help feeling bad for missing an opportunity. Cillian had gone out this morning, and I hadn't even noticed. That meant I had the whole house to myself, during which I could have smashed a window and run.

If I'd had the balls.

Cillian then pulls a stunning navy blue dress out of its cover and holds it up against me. He nods approvingly, admiring what he sees in such a way that my skin starts to crawl all over again. Then he holds it as if he's handing it over and tells me to try it on.

'Right now?' I ask, discomfort making my body tense.

'Not right in front of me,' he says. 'I'm not a monster.'

'How did you know my size?'

'I measured you.'

A weird taste fills my mouth. Hate, maybe. 'When?'

'The other night. While you were sleeping.'

I snatch the dress from him and exit the room, agreeing to try on this 'gift' just to get away from him. Who the hell does he think he is? Why does he think it's okay to take measurements of a woman while she sleeps? If I wasn't already creeped out before, this is enough to push me over the edge. I just don't want to imagine what would happen if I told him I don't want the dress, but there is one lingering question...

What event does he want me to wear it for?

IT QUICKLY BECOMES DISGUSTINGLY apparent that Cillian intends to replicate the other night.

The atmosphere hasn't changed, except now I'm in a tight, navy dress that accents my ample cleavage. The music is no different, and the lighting is the same. It's like he's literally trying to give himself a second chance after I already told him I wasn't ready to kiss him. I should have told him the truth.

That there could be nothing worse than *ever* kissing him.

But there is one thing that's wildly different from last time, and I'm not talking about the dress (in different circumstances, I might actually like the damn thing). Cillian's hand is reaching out to me as he offers a slight, almost princelike bow and asks me to dance.

'Actually,' I say, then freeze when noticing the upset in his eyes. I rummage through my brain to think of something – anything – to say that isn't a direct rejection. 'My chest is feeling a little tight. Would you mind if we go outside?'

'Oh. Is it the dress?'

'Don't think so.'

'Something wrong with the food?'

'Definitely not.'

'Then why can't we dance?'

'Please.' I stand up and shoot past Cillian, over-playing the drama of my fictional condition. This always seems to work around guys – nobody wants to kiss a woman who's struggling to breathe, and even if *he* does, I'll pretend I'm ready to throw up. Simple.

I make it to the front door and wait there for Cillian to open it. Much to my surprise, he passes by and heads for the long glass wall in the living room instead. There he produces a key, slides back a piece of plastic that covers the keyhole, then unlocks it and slides open a large pane of glass to grant access to the pool area.

Stunned, I go past him and step outside. The whole time I've been a prisoner here, I had no idea these windows opened without smashing right through them. That's something worth adding to my list of potential escape routes.

Outside, the cool air hits me like a bullet. I shiver, feel Cillian moving in to put his arms around me. I pretend not to notice and walk forward until I'm standing over the pool, where the moonlight bounces off in dazzling beauty. The bulbs on the surrounding walls look like fairy lights. It's actually beautiful, but I'm too scared to comment on it.

Behind me, Cillian pulls the door (window, whatever) shut. It glides into place with only a little sound. He comes to stand at my side, his reflection in the rippling water appearing beside mine. Before he can beat me to it, I cover my own arms and stifle a shiver.

'Are you cold?' he asks.

'Yes, but I like it.'

'Want me to get you something to wear?'

'No, it's fine.'

'I'll get you something to wear.'

I roll my eyes like some entitled bitch being treated like a lady on a first date. Cillian goes back inside and emerges seconds later with a blanket. Before he puts it around me, his eyes linger on my figure a little too long. My shivers intensify. He licks his lips.

'The blanket,' I remind him.

'Sorry.'

Cillian drapes it around me and rubs my arms. I pull away. He's *really* trying tonight. So hard that I'm already making up excuses for the rest of the evening. Is this something I'll have to do forever? Will he ever take no for an answer?

'Is it something I said?' he asks, stuffing his hands into his pockets.

'No. I mean... yes. I'm just not ready for a boyfriend yet.'

'Then why did you come here with me?'

My head turns of its own volition. 'Is that a serious question?'

'Obviously.'

'You invited me here to take care of me.'

'You were aware of the subtext.'

Subtext? SUBTEXT? What the hell does that even mean? The only reason I came here in the first place was because I had no other option. If I remember rightly, he was the one who talked *me* into coming here. He's the one keeping *me* here against my will. And don't even get me started on what happened to Manuel and Isabella when I asked for help.

'I'm really tired of trying so hard,' he says, turning to face me.

'Then stop trying so hard.'

'Is that a hint?'

'What? No—'

My words are cut off when he places his hands on my shoulders and pulls me in for a kiss. Again. He's stronger than me by far, so his lips actually touch mine before I can even do anything about it. The stubble grazes my upper lip, his breath already hot on my mouth, so I place my hands on his chest and push as hard as I can.

It does nothing.

'Come on,' he says. 'Stop fighting it so hard.'

'I don't want to kiss you,' I tell him firmly, still resisting.

'That's a lie, and you know it.'

'Please don't...'

In the struggle, I push a little too hard. In doing so, my balance escapes me. I step back, my foot sliding off the edge of the pool. Before I know it, the feeling of weightlessness seizes me as I fall. The water is shockingly cold, my breath ripped from me by its icy hand. I scream – at least, I think I do, but it might just be a soundless cry – then reach for the side of the pool. In an instant, Cillian's hand finds mine. He heaves me out of the water with terrifying strength.

Is it weird that I want to thank him for saving me?

Is it even weirder that he's staring daggers at me?

'Look what you did, you silly cow!' he screams, his eyes alight with fury. 'I spent hundreds on that dress, not to mention the time it took to measure you and go to buy it. Then you go and throw your-self into all that chlorine!'

Shivering, terrified, and stunned, all I can do is stare.

'What, you don't have anything to say?' he barks.

'I didn't... You tried to...'

'Don't even think about blaming me. You messed up. Big time.'

With that, he turns and storms off, shoving open the glass pane so hard that it bounces almost all the way back into position. I turn around just long enough to see if there's a gate to escape through, but by then, he's already back in the doorway.

'Are you coming in, darling?' he asks calmly, as if replaced by another person entirely.

The only thing I can think to do is nod. The water was cold, but when mixed with the chilling breeze, I can't stop my teeth from chattering. All I want now is to get in the warm, change into dry clothes, then get a good night's sleep at the other end of the house.

One thing is for certain though.

This time, I'll be the one locking my door.

Chapter 20
Jason...? Now

As far as the rest of the world is concerned, I *am* Jason.

I have his house keys, his car keys, and even the wallet his murderous bitch of a wife decided to leave behind. I even have his phone and laptop, the latter of which he shares with Daisy. No, actually, not shares.

Shared.

I try not to think about it while sitting behind the steering wheel. For now, it's best to look forward rather than back. Try to ignore what happened and figure out how I'm going to deal with it. It's already been decided that I'm going to enter that house at some point.

It's just a matter of when.

The owner comes and goes, but when he does go, he doesn't go for long. Daisy, on the other hand, is yet to even show her face at all. I know she's in there though. She can't go on hiding forever. Not after what she did to Jason.

Not after killing my brother.

Chapter 21
Daisy, Now

ONCE AGAIN, Cillian's entire personality has altered with a sunrise.

This time, he isn't bribing me with a breakfast spread or a dress I'm too proud to admit is beautiful, but has instead checked the progress of my rhinoplasty, told me it's healing well, and then invited me to come and relax with him downstairs to watch a film.

'Today?' I ask. 'In the middle of the day?'

'Is that a problem?'

'No, it's just... What kind of film?'

'Whatever you like. As long as it's not a kids' film.'

I hesitantly agree – my schedule isn't exactly bursting at the seams today – then get changed while he goes to set everything up. Before leaving the room, my eye catches the greenish-yellow hues of the grass in the fields outside, and I dream of life outside these walls. That's something I miss about films: the magic of being able to take you to faraway worlds.

That's what gives me the idea of watching something set in a different world. It's definitely a technicality on being a kids' film, but I head downstairs and suggest we watch Marvel's *Guardians of the Galaxy*. It's an easy space adventure suitable for every age, with plenty of humour and an incredible soundtrack. Jason used to make me watch them, but they grew on me very much over time. Now, it's like a comfort blanket.

'Isn't that a little bit... young?' Cillian asks.

'Trust me, if you don't mind light-hearted fun, then you'll have a good time.'

'Is it at least realistic?'

'Not even a little.' I laugh.

Cillian is wary – that much shows in the scrunching of his face – but he hits the button, and the blinds pull across the glass wall. Although I suppose now they've proven themselves to be actual doors. The room drowns in darkness as the TV takes a few seconds to turn on and adjust itself, a beacon of light in the pitch-black. It illuminates the two sofas, where Cillian is most likely going to want to cuddle with me. I prevent that before it needs a cure.

'Mind if I lie out on one of these?' I ask, pointing. 'My back hurts.'

'That should be fine. Do you need a massage?'

'No, it might make it even worse to tamper with it.'

'If you say so.'

We sit down to enjoy the film, with me stretching out on my back and him perching almost regally on the opposite sofa, one arm spread out across the back cushion like he was hugging an invisible woman, the other resting in his lap. One leg is up and resting horizontally across the other knee, making him look like he's posing rather than actually comfortable.

The film starts with a great song-and-dance moment. I glance at Cillian to see if he's already sucked into it like the rest of the world was when it first came out, but there's not so much as a smile. Over time, he grows bored and likes to prove it by making idle conversation about things that have nothing to do with the film. I give him one-word answers, hoping it serves as a strong enough hint that I'm actually interested in what we're watching.

More than that, really: I *need* to invest in a world outside of our own.

My mental health depends on it.

A while into the film, however, I just can't help joining him. There's a scene where the lead actor (Chris Pratt) goes to some kind of space prison where he's stripped and hosed down with some oddly coloured goo. He's furious, his muscular, naked chest heaving up and down as he stares through the camera in a way that makes every part of my body tingle. No matter how many times I see it, a small 'mmm' sound always makes its way out of my mouth.

Then, the scene pauses.

The music cuts dead.

It takes me a second to understand what's happened. Sitting halfway up to look at Cillian, I ask what's going on. All I see is the TV light flaring up his eyes as he stares at me like there's no emotion in him whatsoever. Except for anger, that is.

'Did you say something?' he asks.

'No. I don't think so, anyway.'

'Are you sure?'

'Not really... Maybe?'

'Sounded to me like you're attracted to this man.'

I hesitate, and then it clicks. 'Who, Chris Pratt?'

'Is that the actor's name?'

'Yeah.'

'Then yes, Chris Pratt.'

Needless to say, I'm speechless. Cillian is obviously upset that I could find another man attractive, but is this really something worth shying away from? Believe it or not, we don't have a relationship, and the man I admire is nothing more than an actor on a screen.

'It's just physical admiration,' I explain. 'I'm sure you find women attractive.'

'Only you.'

The hairs prick on the back of my neck. 'Thank you. Should we keep watching?'

'What if I don't want to any more?'

'Then... that's okay.'

'Yes, it is.'

Cillian pauses in the silence, long enough for me to see the glistening of sweat on his creased forehead and hear the heavy breathing that can only be from a man trying his best not to smash up an entire room in a blind rage. Then, he leaps out of his seat and tosses the remote on to my lap before storming out. As he leaves me in stunned silence, I catch one last comment while he storms out of the room – two words that make me shudder at the very sound of them.

'Fucking whore.'

The door slams. I jump out of my skin.

Then I'm alone.

Upstairs, across the hall from my bedroom, is a reading room. It's a cute little space with a vast library that covers three entire walls from floor to ceiling. A lot of the books are non-fiction, but there is a space for fantasy. It's not my usual style – I tend to go for thrillers, but my mind is chaotic enough in the middle of this madness.

There are two armchairs, both deep and comfortable, and a wide window that lets in a ton of light. It's the perfect place to relax, which is only made better by the speaker system in which you can connect to your phone via Bluetooth.

If only I had my phone...

Cillian still has it, and I dare not ask him to

return it. Honestly, I still feel as though I've done something wrong after watching that Marvel film (which I did not finish). Before the credits rolled, my irritation made me give up on it, so I came up here to stare blankly at the inside of an open book instead.

I didn't know *this* would make me so uncomfortable.

The shuffling sound started the moment I sat down. Cillian is out in the hallway, pacing up and down. I lick my dry lips and listen as he mumbles to himself like a crazy person. It's hard to hear exactly what he's saying, but every time he gets closer to this end of the hall, I distinctly hear his complaints of what happened last night.

'... Chris Pratt... absolute joke... whore.'

Look, nobody likes being called a whore, but I didn't even sleep with somebody to warrant it. I only mentioned that the actor on the film was attractive because Cillian happened to pick up on a primal sound I made when seeing a muscly chest.

I try to settle into the book, but the voice keeps coming back.

'... just keep your legs together... bloody filthy...'

Once more, I try to let his angry mumbling wash over me. Water off a duck's back, I tell myself, turning the book back a page to start again. This time, I manage to make it three pages in before I stop to realise how much of a miracle that is.

Then I glance towards the door.

He's there.

'I have a surprise for you,' he says eerily, staring right into my soul as he lingers behind the door frame. Then he shifts his body, and I think he's going to pull out a bouquet of flowers or something cringeworthy like that. But his hands come into view. They're empty.

'Oh?' I say.

'Come downstairs.'

'Right now?'

'You heard me.'

Cillian vanishes from sight. I hesitantly close the book and place it on the small side table, then push myself out of the comfortable armchair and start to follow my captor downstairs. It's not until I reach the banister in the hall that I realise...

My hands are shaking like crazy.

I STEP into a living room that looks no different than it did an hour ago, but Cillian expects a reaction. He stands there beside me, staring, expecting some sort of reaction I don't know how to conjure. What am I supposed to be looking at? What exactly is he waiting for?

'I don't understand,' I say softly, trying not to sound as frustrated as I feel.

'Isn't it obvious?' He gestures at the TV. 'I'm giving you what you want.'

'O...kay.'

Cillian invites me to sit down, and it wouldn't be wise to decline. I go for the same sofa as last time, only now he knocks my feet aside casually with the back of his hand and tells me to scoot over. Pulling my legs back and hugging my knees, I can't help feeling that slight prick of fear all over again – the discomfort of having him near.

Then he puts the TV on.

Suddenly, I understand.

What I'm looking at is a long list of films on a streaming service. I study them all one by one, trying my hardest to find the common connection between them all. It doesn't take long – I've read the titles of three different films before it clicks.

They all star Chris Pratt.

'Thought I would give you what you want,' Cillian says, resting a hand on my foot. It lingers there a little too long, enough to make me feel like taking my chances and just running into the fields outside, but I quickly come to my senses. 'You want to stare at another man like he's some kind of sexual object, you go right ahead. But at the very least, I want to be here to watch you. To see what makes you tick, Daisy, so I can strive to be the same.'

Speechless. That's the only word for it. Even though he's gazing at me, I dare not look him in the eye. All I can think to do is watch the TV, ask him to start the marathon, then slowly pull my feet away from his grip. Unfortunately, he's on to me, sliding his hand forward to ensure he can keep his skin connected to mine.

But that's not the only problem.

Twenty minutes into *Jurassic World*, his eyes haven't left me.

His stare is so creepy it makes me itch. My skin pricks into goosebumps, and it takes a fight to keep myself from shuddering. I'm strongly resisting the urge to let my head turn even slightly towards him because then we'll be eye to eye.

Exactly how he wants it.

But what can I really do about it?

'You look so beautiful,' he says calmly.

I don't get a chance to respond before his hand slides up my leg. I sit bolt upright and inch away, but then his fingers are between my legs. A shiver bites right through me as I slap his hand away. Cillian's eyes widen. My heart starts pounding. There's a moment of silence.

Then he goes for the kiss.

I pull away, but he leans closer. My back is to the arm of the sofa, and he climbs atop me. Between my legs, he starts to thrust, his lips finding my neck. I tell him no. He doesn't listen – only grows firmer in his approach. Panic sears through me as I try to pull a knee up to get him out from between my legs. But he's strong – *so* strong – and he won't let me do it.

'Cillian,' I say, the word coming out hard and nasty. 'Stop.'

'Just pretend I'm him,' he says, sounding lost in the moment. 'Call me Chris.'

'No, Cillian. I don't want this.'

Then his lips touch mine. A spike of adrenaline. Seizing of the muscles. I retreat into myself as he cups my breast. My hand snaps out in a heartbeat, hitting him so softly as if I'm too scared to hurt him because I know what he can do to me. Then, after a moment's hesitation, I strike again. Hard, this time. Hard enough to make him sit up and gaze at me.

'I don't want to be touched,' I tell him firmly, making it a clear, concise statement.

'You... don't?'

'No. Please get off me.'

'This must mean...' He drifts into another world. 'No...'

The room is so quiet that – even with the film blaring in the background – I can hear myself panting through the panic. Cillian doesn't move an inch, the gears turning behind his dead eyes while he decides whether to take it further. In this moment, I'm terrified that he can take control – he's stronger than me, and there's nowhere to go. That silence drags on for an eternity, my breath caught in my throat.

Until he finally gets off.

A moment later, he storms out of the room.

Again.

Chapter 22
Daisy, Then

NOBODY HAD EVER TOLD me the real weight of a human body.

But Jason was no normal human.

Bearlike in his size, he had always frightened the ever-loving hell out of me. After the very first time he shouted at me and I saw that aggressive nature buried deep behind his eyes, I'd become immediately aware of his strength and physical stature. Perhaps that was why I'd always felt so vulnerable around him. So helpless.

Right up until the moment he died.

There was something of a power shift after that. I wouldn't go so far as to say I felt strong, but doing what I'd done made me realise I wasn't so helpless after all. Maybe in time, that feeling would be shelved by someone more powerful than even Jason, but for now, all I had to think about was getting this body somewhere quiet.

And I knew just where to put it.

Jason had taken me there before. It was so secluded, the trees so tall and dense that it was dark even in the daytime. Now, long after the stroke of midnight, I was willing to bet it was impossible to see a thing. That made it the perfect place to do it.

There was nowhere better to bury him.

It made me feel disgusting, of course. This was the man I loved. But that feeling was something I had to stifle as I lugged his body into the back seat of the car (he wouldn't fit in the boot) and drove through town to his final resting place. My body was tensed the whole time, wound up so tight that I was giving myself a headache. I was so incredibly paranoid that the police would stop me, even though it had never happened in my life.

Because if I got stopped tonight, my life was over.

Just like Jason's was.

By sheer stroke of luck, I made it to the woods. I parked behind the bushes and got to work on dragging Jason between the trees, trying my hardest not to look at his lifeless face. There was a light on my phone, but it stayed off until I made it to the right spot, where I left my husband and went back to the car for the shovel I'd been smart enough to bring.

Then I returned.

And started digging.

It's not that I was completely emotionless, but it hadn't quite hit me yet. Jason was dead, and I was disposing of his body. It occurred to me that I could tell the police what happened – that all I'd done was defend myself – but even bringing him out to the woods made me look guilty as hell. There was no way I would get away with this. I would face jail time for sure. Life, probably, and that just wasn't going to happen.

When the deed was done, I returned to my car and drove as fast as I could back into town.

But I didn't get very far.

Those were the first set of headlights I'd seen that night, and I lost my breath when I saw them. Not because someone had seen me on the road but because the Jeep had additional lights. Four on the top, blindingly bright. There was only one man around here with lights like those.

And we knew each other.

Very well.

———

I PULLED over to the side of the road. It would look more suspicious if I didn't. The Jeep stopped, too, not far from me. The man got out, a black silhouette coming my way. I was suddenly hyper-aware of how strange it was for me to be out there at that time of night, and a good excuse couldn't come to me fast enough.

Before I knew it, it was too late.

Freddy was at my car door.

I rolled down the window and plastered on my best, most genuine smile. It didn't get me very far – he was usually very good to me, but right now, he had a face like thunder. His features were all creased up, like he was holding in the deepest pain known to man.

Imagine if he knew the truth.

That I'd just killed his brother.

'Daisy? What's going on?' he asked, peering through my car window.

'What do you mean?'

'It's two in the morning.'

'So?'

'So why are you out and driving around?'

Maybe it was the mania of having just killed my own husband, but the ridiculousness of the situation could have also been a factor. There was nothing to say – no excuse to be made – so when I opened my mouth to give some kind of excuse, all that came out was a deep, hysterical laugh so hard it felt like it would rupture my stomach.

'What's funny?' he asked as I continued to cackle. 'Daisy?'

I took ages to come to my senses, and by then, I'd thought of something smart to say – a good enough reason for being out here while also providing an explanation as to why nobody would hear from Jason for the next few days. Or, you know... forever.

'Jason didn't come home from the pub tonight. It closed a couple of hours ago, and he isn't picking up his phone. It's not like him at all, so I came out looking for him. You haven't seen him by any chance, have you?'

Freddy stared, squinting. It was clear he didn't believe me.

'All you did was come straight here?' he asked.

'Yep. No sign of him yet.'

'But the pub is that way.' He pointed in the opposite direction.

'Yes, but when he wasn't there, I decided to try the next one.'

'How about your legs?'

'What about them?'

'They're caked in dirt.'

My body flushed with cold then. I panicked, looked down at my legs, and he was right. How had I missed that? Anyone would think it was my first time burying a dead body. Naturally, I fumbled for an excuse, stuttering like a bloody idiot.

'Ah, that was from my garden. Lawn, I mean. I fell. Stupid darkness. That was when I was going for the car. Wish it wasn't so dark.' I laughed so awkwardly that even a blind man could tell I was lying through my teeth. Hell, a blind man could even see the dirt on my trousers. There was so much of it that I hated myself for not having so much as dusted myself off.

Freddy didn't match my laugh. All he did was look me up and down. It was like he knew I was lying but needed to find a way to prove it. As if he needed more evidence – all he had to do was look in the boot and find the shovel.

'Shall I try him?' he asked.

'Try...?'

'Calling him.'

'Oh. If you want. You'll have the same luck.'

Freddy backed away from my car and pulled out his phone. Suddenly, I was all clenched up and praying his phone wasn't still in the car. How would I explain that? How on earth could I talk my way out of that one? I waited impatiently for the phone to ring, Freddy looking me all over while he tried his best to contact Jason.

But he never got through.

'No answer,' he said, hanging up.

'Makes sense.'

'Did you have some kind of argument?'

'No? Why do you ask?' I suddenly went from cold to hot.

'Because that would explain him vanishing.'

'Oh. No.' Shaking my head, trying to sound convincing. 'Nothing like that.'

'And he seemed fine beforehand?'

'Totally fine. I'm really worried.'

'It does seem out of character...'

Freddy rested a hand on the door and looked up and down the road. It almost felt like he was about to do something – perhaps lean in and strangle me, squeezing the truth out of me. God knows I would cave in an instant. Lying never was my strong suit.

'All right,' he said. 'Let me know when you hear from him.'

'Will do. Same for you.'

'Definitely.'

'Take care.'

Just like that, Freddy left me on the side of the road, got in his Jeep, and drove away. I sat there for a while, faking a smile as he passed me and giving it a minute before I started driving. I badly needed to collect myself – to steady my breathing. I may have got away with murder for now, and Freddy had no idea I'd just buried his brother in the woods. But before long, he would put two and two together, quickly figuring out why he'd seen me that night and why I was really caked in dirt. Not much got past him.

It was no wonder, really.

He was always the brighter of the two brothers.

I RUSHED HOME AFTER THAT, ran inside the house, locked the door, and collapsed against it with my head in my hands. My husband was dead

– *dead* – and it was one hundred per cent my fault. Had he bullied me into defending myself? Of course he had, but that didn't give me the right to take his life, stabbing him repeatedly while he wondered where the hell that strength had come from. He wasn't alone, either – I'd been as confused as him.

Warm, salty tears rolling into the corner of my mouth, I continued to sob. It was only a matter of time until that body was found. I could see it now; people would start to notice that Jason was quiet for so long, Freddy would start thinking back to the last time anyone had heard from him, and then the official investigation would start. I tried to picture myself in one of those police interview rooms, crying my eyes out while pleading for my husband's safe return. Acting had never come naturally to me, so of course, I began to panic.

But it was just a case of one step at a time.

Yes, that was it. The key to my sanity. All I had to do was slow down, breathe deeply, think of putting one foot in front of the other. I couldn't just sit around the house waiting for the cops to turn up. Something had to be done.

I had to leave town for good.

With that in mind, stage one began to make

itself very clear. All I had to do was pack, as if I was going on holiday but with no intention of returning. Somehow, I peeled myself off the hallway floor and made it all the way upstairs. I sifted through my clothes – some of which Jason had bought for me, and it tore me apart to shove those aside – and grabbed only what was necessary. There were some cosmetics on the side, a phone charger, the phone itself, and some medications I could probably live without. It all went straight on to the bed, where I took a deep breath and then started to stuff it all into the open suitcase.

It was hard to believe I was fleeing my life.

If only I had done this sooner.

Either way, Jason would no longer be there.

Shoving that thought way down into the pit of my stomach, I wrestled with the suitcase to close it, then realised I didn't need that much. I'd always been minimalist, so why change that now? Opting for a backpack instead, I tore some things out of the case, made the transfer, then took one last, long look around the home I'd lived in with my husband.

It was time to say goodbye.

I called for a taxi next, sat in the back, and headed to literally anywhere besides here. The whole time, all I could think about was how much I wanted to change my face. Anything to not be recognised while also dealing with the problem of my hideous features. That was something that'd been drilled into me for a long time by my dearly beloved...

My dearly *departed*.

No, I had to shake off those thoughts. There was a whole future to look forward to – all my possessions condensed into a single bag and a long, open road ahead of me. It wasn't lost on me that Freddy would try to pursue me, either. He and his brother were incredibly close, so it was only a matter of hours. I would have to think of excuses and lies to get myself out of trouble, which I was already working on. It started with what happened the night Jason went missing – what I would tell the police had happened during those late hours.

You've already heard those lies.

Chapter 23
Daisy, Now

A WHOLE DAY comes and goes. Cillian doesn't say a word to me the whole time, and I've gone hungry. He hasn't offered me food, and I dare not ask for it. Not just because I feel scared and vulnerable but because I'm so ridiculously angry at him that I won't give him the satisfaction.

I would rather starve.

That doesn't mean I don't encounter him from time to time, however. We've passed each other on the stairs, where he brushes past me like a bull charging through a flapping red flag. I've gone into one of the bathrooms right after he's come out of it, only to have him pull the door shut, mumble something angrily under his breath, then march down the hall. The last time I saw him, he even knocked a scalding cup of coffee from my hand. Thankfully, nobody got hurt. Not unless you count my wounded pride.

This morning is slightly different though. Cillian has a problem – that much is clear from the swinging of his arms – but this time, it doesn't seem to be with me. I can tell from the way I've become invisible to him. The way he's leaning over the kitchen counter with such intense concentration that he hasn't even noticed me enter the room.

I want to ask him about it. I want to know what exactly has him so fed up, but I'm scared he'll tell me. What if it's the same problem as always – that he wants me so badly, but the feeling isn't mutual? There are only so many times I can reject his advances. To be honest, I'm terrified that next time will be the one where he won't stop. That a slap won't be enough.

Rather than satisfy my need to know, I leave the room in the direction of the stairs. But then his voice stops me in my tracks. It's not fear that gets me this time though.

It's curiosity.

'You couldn't have said that on the phone?' he snaps angrily, and it takes a while to realise he's not talking to me. He must have made a call. 'You had to send it by text? An abrupt one at that. Not exactly fair, is it?'

Naturally, I take a few steps back towards the kitchen, tiptoeing across the floorboards so as not to make them creak. I can see Cillian's reflection in the spotless stainless-steel oven across the way. With his back turned, he can't see me.

Thank God.

'That's not the point!' he yells, replicating that same tone he had only yesterday. 'No, I have a life to live. Don't you think a little bit of warning could have gone a long way? Yes. That's right. This is going to continue being a problem, I can feel it.'

I won't lie – this little insight into Cillian's personal woes is fascinating to me. I've only ever seen him as this successful, prolific surgeon with a somewhat aggressive mental health problem. If I'd known he had his own issues going on behind closed doors, I'd have had questions. I *do* have questions.

And I intend to ask them.

It's wise to let the phone call end, but it takes a while.

First, I have to hear him bitch and moan about how unfair it is. Actually, he sounds like a petulant child, digging in his heels until he can get his own way. Although from the sounds of it, he doesn't get it. If his complaining doesn't suggest that enough, his slamming of the kitchen cupboards does. It's hard enough that I jump, even from the hallway.

As soon as he's done, he hangs up and sits at the kitchen island, dragging a stool across the tiles with an ear-piercing shriek. I can hear him breathing, so heavily stressed that it's making the air tense even out here. I want to know more, of course, but how can I do that without making it obvious I've been out here this whole time?

I need to retreat first.

Back up the stairs I go, treading lightly so as not to be heard. When I reach the top, I turn around and bound back down, making as much noise as possible. Cillian must have heard me because by the time I reach the kitchen, he's already spun around. Now, he's staring at me with deep, sorrowful eyes. Not the eyes of a man who wants forgiveness.

But a man who wants my help.

'What's wrong with *you*?' I ask, acting as though there's been no ill will between us – like he wasn't dangerously close to sexually assaulting me less than twenty-four hours ago. 'You look like someone ran over your cat.'

'And then pissed on the corpse,' he adds.

'So what's wrong?'

'You wouldn't understand.'

'Try me.'

It's one of my more feeble attempts to suck up to him, but it's never been more necessary than it is right now. I head into the kitchen, pull up a stool with a large space between us, then lean forward with my elbows on the counter. I watch him after asking again what's wrong, and for the first time, *he's* the one avoiding looking *me* in the eye.

'It's my dad,' he says.

I have no idea why that comment sucker-punches me. I've never really thought about Cillian having a life before – no fears, just desires – so to know he has a dad knocks me for six. Seeing the miserable look on his face confuses me, too.

It's like he actually has emotions other than rage.

'What's wrong with your dad?' I probe.

'He's not a nice man.'

'Why not?'

'He's... harsh. Abrupt. Controlling.'

So it's genetic. 'Sorry to hear that. Families can be tough. The best thing you can do is try to keep your head up, carry on with your life, and try to give them as few triggers as possible. They can't get to you if you don't expose yourself.'

Stressing now, Cillian rakes a hand through his perfect hair. 'Easier said than done.'

'Oh, come on. It can't be that hard to keep your head down.'

'Trust me, you have no idea how much he can ruin my life.'

'I'm having a hard time believing you. Look around.' I wave around the room with my hand, but my point extends beyond that. 'You've got an amazing career, all of this to yourself, and so much respect in your profession that nobody would dare—'

'He's coming to stay, Daisy.'

A long pause. It stretches on. Cillian won't look at me, and that's a good thing. A well of hope opens within me. If his old man is coming to stay, that brings a ton of whole new avenues for escape. Especially if he's as scared of his own father as he seems.

'Why are you smiling?' he asks.

'I didn't realise I was.'

'You don't know how serious this is. For us.'

'What do you mean?'

Cillian pushes away his stool and begins to pace the kitchen. I admit it's not exactly a comfort to have him walking up and down and around me, but while he's this stressed, I have a chance to be the kind friend. And we don't try to rape kind friends, do we?

'Let's just say he likes to put a dampener on fun,' he says through gritted teeth. 'Seriousness is all he has, and it poisons the air in every single room he's in. You think things can be stressful now? Wait until he's here.'

At least he recognises how stressful it is. If only he understood he's been the cause of this upset. 'I'm sure he's not that bad. Why don't you just try telling him when he's upset you?'

'And give him ammunition?'

'Wow, how bad *is* this guy?'

'I wasn't exaggerating.'

'Okay, so let me talk to him.'

Cillian stops. Turns. Stares. 'Why?'

'So I can tell him what a great guy you are. Think about it...' I go to him and look him in the eye, attempting to be as convincing as possible. 'Give me a moment alone with him, and I'll tell him to ease off you a little. I can charm him, make him warm to me, then sprinkle in some details about how he should leave you alone. Wouldn't that help?'

'It might.'

'Well, there you go.'

'It's just that...' Cillian pauses as if to taste his next thought, then shakes his head like he's spitting it out. 'No. That's not a good idea. The less contact you have with him, the better. It might even be best for you to stay in your room.'

My mouth hangs open. 'For how long?'

'We'll decide that just before he gets here.'

'Right. When does he get here?'

'Tomorrow.'

I nod, then make an excuse to leave the room. If Cillian's father is coming tomorrow, then I have a whole day to think about what I'm going to say – how I'm going to convince him to open the front door and let me go. Maybe even drive me into town and let me go. At least one person in this godforsaken bloodline has to treat me like a human being.

They can't all be monsters...

Can they?

It's only after this morning that I start to notice things.

Throughout the day, Cillian starts to act a little less comfortable around the house. It seems like our little 'altercation' is behind us, but there's still something wrong. Something that extends far beyond me and him. Maybe even beyond the issues with his father.

First, I'm only now seeing the pictures on the walls. I guess I've always seen them, but it's only really now that I've actually stopped to study them. I see him now – the man standing beside Cillian in family photographs. They're equal in height, except his father holds it with slightly more weight. His cheeks are fleshed out behind grey stubble, the hairline receded and a lingering confidence in his eyes. It's a tiger-like confidence, as if he could finish you in an instant. If those peepers match the ones in the photos, I understand Cillian's discomfort.

But there's so much more to it than that.

There are letters around the house, and they're addressed to a Tony White. The man in question, I presume, although there's no reference to his wife – Cillian's mother. If I think back far enough, however, I could have sworn he said his mother passed away.

Probably took her own life to get away from this psycho family.

I shake my head at the sick thought and continue walking up the hallway. Before I know it, I'm pushing open doors I've never opened before. *Seeing* things I didn't even know to look for. There are more bedrooms, more wardrobes, and more possessions. The more I see, the less this house feels like Cillian, and the more it feels like he's as much a guest as I am.

It's the letters that seal the thought.

Not the ones I found earlier, but the ones on the desk in the biggest bedroom I've seen in my entire life. It's an ugly, oaken thing that occupies a whole corner the same way an unsightly, bulking furnace takes up a basement. There are pages everywhere, with headers on each letter from medical companies I've never heard of. Those are also addressed to Tony.

Tony.

Not Cillian.

As I start to sift through them, the truth slowly starts coming to light. I can't read through them fast enough – my hands shuffling through them all as my eyes dance back and forth across the paper. My heart is about to burst out of my chest like an alien from one of those old sci-fi films, the deadly reality of my situation becoming quickly and devastatingly apparent.

Then, as Cillian appears in the doorway and sighs – like he knows this is the end of our journey – I slowly drop the letters and take a step back. Stunned, I back away towards the window and try with all my strength to talk through the shock.

Because this isn't his house at all. It's Tony's.

And Cillian was never a surgeon at all.

Chapter 24
Daisy, Now

'No need to look so surprised,' Cillian says, like it's all one big joke.

But I *am* surprised. Absolutely bloody blown away, even. How did I not see this before? Why did it take this much snooping to finally understand the situation I'm in? It makes me wonder... if I saw this before he mentioned his father, would I have put it together then?

My back hits the windowsill, and I stop dead. Cillian comes inside the room and sits on the bed, resting his hands on his knees. While I'm still too stunned to speak, he heaves a second big sigh and lowers his head. I'm not ready to buy that he feels regret.

Which is fine because he isn't about to pretend.

'It was only a matter of time until you figured it out,' he says. 'And there, now you know why I so badly hate the idea of Dad coming home after a long business trip. When I said he's controlling, what I meant to say was that he has the final say on what happens in his house.'

I'm still having trouble accepting it. My memory is quickly rewinding through these past few days, highlighting images from when he dressed my wounds, gave me aftercare advice, even removed the cast from my nose. I can't make sense of it.

'How?' I ask in a meek, frightened little whimper. 'How did you know what to do?'

'You mean medically?'

I nod rapidly.

'My father has been a plastic surgeon for over thirty years. You tend to learn a thing or two when living under the same roof as somebody like that. I've heard him talk about it more than a few times. In fact, he never shuts up about it. As if his job means more to him than his own son. Can you really blame me for hating him?'

'What about you? You live here?'

'I didn't lie about that, Daisy.'

'But you're not a surgeon?'

'Nope. Don't even have a job.'

My memory is going at it again, dropping the pieces it's supposed to be fitting together. There's something else. Something that won't stay down. 'But I met you. You performed the surgery. I met you both before and after.'

'No.' Cillian shakes his head and scratches his five o'clock shadow. It sounds like a body being dragged through the grass, which makes me think of poor Isabella. 'I didn't perform anything. All I did was happen to be at the clinic cafeteria the morning you came in for your surgery. I only went in there to borrow something from Dad's desk drawer, but I needed something to eat. When I saw you, I... Hmm, it was hard to resist playing make-believe.'

I shake my head now, disbelieving. *Refusing.*

'You performed the surgery itself.'

'Did you see me in theatre?'

'Well... no. But after...?'

'You mean the car park?'

'Yes.'

'I saw you were waiting and had a good idea.' Cillian stands up, walks around the room like he owns the place – which is now very clear he does not. 'A woman badly in need of somewhere to stay, me with a big house and no company whatsoever. It made sense to me. And I know you wouldn't have come with me if you knew I wasn't a surgeon, so I chose to pretend. The rest, as they say, is history.'

A sickening feeling unsettles my stomach. The bitter taste of bile touches my tongue. My hand reaches out behind me as if to look for a way out. Then my eyes follow. All I see through the window is the ground far below. Too far to jump, and no ledge in sight. This is it.

This is where I'm going to die.

'What will your father say?' I ask. 'When he finds out you've kept me here.'

'Please. I didn't keep you here. All I ever did was help you.'

'Against my will.'

'Did you not agree to coming up here?'

'Initially, yes.'

'There you go, then.'

Cillian continues to pace, sometimes coming back to me and other times walking around the enormous, majestic bed complete with bedposts and curtains. A pattern emerges – when he's at the far end of his path, there's enough room for me to reach the door. Only if I'm fast enough, that is. It's hard to say if my legs will let me do it or give out through sheer terror.

I have to be brave. Fake it till you make it, as they say.

'So let me get this straight,' I snap, punching the harsh syllables out like I'm scolding him. 'You're unemployed, living in your father's home, pretended to be a surgeon, invited a patient into your home, and now you're... what? Hoping to keep me here even when your father comes back from his trip? How is that going to work, exactly?'

Cillian stops, his back to me. He's at the far end, so now is a good time to run, but I'm too scared to move. 'I was wondering that myself. It would have been nice if you could help me keep up appearances, but it's getting harder to trust you. For instance, see the attempts you made with Manuel and Isabella. No wonder they had to go.'

'Where did they go, Cillian?' I'm pretty sure I know the answer.

'Isn't it obvious?'

'Say it.'

'They're gone, my love. Dead.'

Disgust rages through me. I feel responsible but can't let that feeling linger. It's not my fault.

This is all his doing. Except I now know for certain that he's capable of murder, and I'm locked in this house with his father coming home soon. Something tells me he isn't going to parade me around in front of the real surgeon, so what will become of me?

I'm too scared to ask.

I simply have to leave.

My eyes dart to the door. The window of opportunity is closing. Cillian still has his back to me, and there's no way of knowing what he'll do if I let him get away with it. I'm already processing what I'll do when I make it through that door – *if* I make it through. All I know is I'll be making use of the living room's glass doors, running for my life and screaming to the heavens until someone comes. All the while, praying Cillian doesn't catch me.

It's now or never. Time to be brave.

Sucking in a deep breath, I fight through the adrenaline and run for the door. Cillian turns then, eyes wide, mouth open. My hand is almost on the door to widen it, but then his thick, manly arm feeds through the gap to stop it. Before I know it, he's shoving me back while blocking my only exit. I hit the floor with an agonising thud, staring up at my captor.

I'm as good as dead.

IT'S NOT GOING to end here.

Not like this.

I've gone through too much to just lie on my back and fall victim to this man's strength. An energetic surge of anger blasts through me. My hands ball into fists. I grit my teeth. Cillian reaches for my hair with a grasping hand, but I swat it away and pull back my knee.

Then kick as hard as I can.

My heel strikes his shin. He cries out in thunderous pain and rushes to nurse it, fury lighting up his eyes like burning coals. Meanwhile, I scramble backwards on my hands until there's a safe distance between us, then push myself to my feet and run for the door again.

This time, it almost works.

It's Cillian's hand that stops me, swinging out ferociously. It only catches me on the shoulder, but it's enough to shoot hot pain right through my shoulder and neck. The adrenaline quickly numbs it, I regain my balance, then slip out the door.

'Come back here, you little bitch!'

Sprinting for the end of the hall, I hear his footsteps behind me. Cillian is far bigger, far stronger than I am, but I have to try. I make it all the way to the stairs and start running down them, terror making the hairs on my nape point like little daggers.

But those footsteps are closer now.

Too close.

I feel his hand shoot out before I see it. My feet give way again. I lunge for a grip on the banister but find no purchase. All I feel is weightlessness that stretches on for an age before gravity yanks me back down and batters my body with every roll and tumble down the stairs.

When I finally hit the bottom, I'm too beat up to move. There's ringing in my ears, my vision blurred as the world spins. It's funny what happens to you when fear and pain work together; I'm thinking about Jason and all the times he made me feel small, about the surgery that might have been messed up with my fall down the great staircase. What would he say if he could see me now? I bet he'd be laughing.

It's not Jason who comes for me though. It's Cillian, stomping slowly down the stairs in such intimidating showmanship that my lip is quivering. I'm too scared to move and probably couldn't if I tried – the pain is just too much.

'You were warned,' he says, hanging his head in disappointment. 'You had your chance.'

Then, just like that, his fist rockets towards my temple. It somehow moves in slow motion, and the pain echoes through my skull, even as the ringing increases and my eyes close. I'm tired now. *Exhausted.* What I need is to sleep, so I put my head to rest.

Before everything turns black.

I WAKE up cold with an urgent need for exploration after the slow, deliberate opening of my eyes. When I see nothing but black, panic speeds up my heart and tells me I'm blind – Cillian hit me so hard that somehow it compromised my vision – but then my body adjusts to the darkness. Shadows and silhouettes appear in the tangle of light and darkness.

Where am I?

It takes all of my energy to sit up, but I fight through it. My clothes are slightly damp, my skin raised into goosebumps. I shiver uncontrollably and work my way to my feet, holding on to what feels like the corner of some wooden furniture. It sure has the texture of wood, that sawdust-like smell alerting my senses.

It's just so damn *cold*!

My skull is on fire, too. Cillian saw to that. The last memory I have is of him throwing his best right hook at me, a defenceless young woman. Well, defenceless is circumstantial, and young is subjective, but it was unnecessary all the same.

As the shape of the room begins to reveal itself in my adjusting vision, I feel around to see how big a space I'm in. There's something dripping in the corner, and the floor feels hard. Like stone. The walls are craggy and thick, and I walk right through multiple cobwebs while fighting them out of my hair. If not for the glowing outline of a door at the top of the stairs, I would think I was in a well or cave – something like that. But it's obvious now.

I'm in the cellar.

How long does Cillian intend to keep me down here? *Why* is he keeping me here? If he intends to keep me here as his girlfriend, perhaps death would be better suited for me. Although, for all I know, that could also be the plan. When Tony White gets here – owner of the grand home and father of the demented wannabe surgeon – there will only be two things Cillian can do: finally give up and let me go...

Or silence me entirely.

Chapter 25
Daisy, Then

Everything I told you about my past was entirely truthful though. I really did go from town to town looking for somewhere safe to stay. I really was pursued the whole time, although admittedly, it was by Freddy rather than his brother, Jason.

I felt horribly guilty about it, too. Just so we're clear, it wasn't one of those situations where I killed somebody for sport and then tried to flee the scene with another target in mind. I'd loved Jason fully and with all my heart. Those nights in the hotel rooms were filled with nothing but tears, remorse, and regret. Maybe that contributed to my desires for plastic surgery – I was already starting to hate looking in a mirror because all that stared back at me was a killer. The woman with dead eyes who'd killed the man I loved.

No wonder that face needed to change.

By the time I got the details of a plastic surgeon from Chester, the man I'd met in the bar and had used to fill my confidence (even if just a little), it was already decided that my face needed to drastically change. It was a decision forged from the combined issues of my self-confidence, the constant reminder that I was a killer, and – this is the big one – the fact I was on the run from the brother of the man I'd murdered and buried in the woods.

No wonder he was pissed off.

After doing some extensive research online, I finally approached the clinic to enquire about the multiple surgeries. They said Dr. White was away on a trip and that Shelley Brown was going to stand in temporarily. I didn't realise at the time that Dr. White would turn out to be Tony, not Cillian. We all know what happened later.

But everything was looking good. We discussed my need for rhinoplasty and that I didn't want to end up having one of those upturned Barbie noses like most of the young women out there. I agonisingly went over how saggy my chin was and explained the fat needed to be sucked out. My ears – Shelley insisted they didn't need to change, but there was no talking me out of it – were to be downsized and pinned. It was all drastic and very, *very* expensive, but it was a price worth paying if it meant I no longer looked like me.

Now, Shelley did insist that my hopes were set a little too high. Apparently, too many people went in expecting a life-altering change in their appearance, and – although the results were always impressive – they often ended up disappointed. As if they thought people would automatically become attracted to them. That was fine by me because I wasn't going for comfort. Personally, all I wanted was to not look like Daisy Campbell any more.

Was that so much to ask?

Before I knew it, I was in the back seat of yet another taxi. Some things were just impossible to stay off the record, but I thought it was safe in the clinic. Freddy would never be able to get me there, so I felt a little more relaxed about paying by card. Besides, the transaction apparently showed as a discreet nickname on the bank records. The only other thing on my mind was the aftercare – Shelley had insisted somebody be there to take care of me, so I decided to suck it up and make another call to my cousin, confirming Lily would pick me up when the procedure was over. She kindly said it would be fine to come and meet me at the clinic when my surgeries were finished.

Finally, I had something to look forward to.

THE VERY NEXT DAY, I'm in a room with Dr. White's team as they hit me with a series of questions about my health, make me say out loud what I'm there for, and then give me a brief rundown of what to expect from the surgery.

My thoughts had been so occupied by Freddy hunting me down I hadn't taken the time to consider the surgery itself. Now that I was in the clinic, mere minutes away from changing my face forever, my hands were finally starting to shake. I fiddled with my necklace to try to hide my nerves, but the surgeon picked up on it.

'Try to relax,' he said, smiling while the light glistened off his bald head.

'Easy for you to say. You're not the one getting chopped and changed.'

'We do this every day of our lives. You're going to be fine.'

'Do you ever make mistakes?'

'It happens, but that's life.'

'How brutally honest.'

'Legally, I'm not allowed to lie to you.' The surgeon sighs, still smiling, then puts the clipboard on the desk and wheels back. 'Listen, we have an empty schedule for today, so why don't you go and take a breather? De-stress. There's a cafeteria downstairs, so help yourself – it's all complimentary – then come back in about an hour, and we'll take good care of you.'

I smiled gratefully, took his directions to the cafeteria, then headed straight for it. I was told not to eat much, and my unsettled tummy wouldn't have allowed food anyway, so I just took a bottle of water from the fridge and turned to walk away.

That was the first time I saw him.

He was a tall guy, thin but in one of those slick, athletic ways. His jaw was so tight that I wondered if he got a staff discount for surgeries, and his face had that sexy, pointed look to it. As if that wasn't enough to make me swoon, his sapphire eyes were piercing and then pinned me down with something between a smile and a bad-boy look.

'I'm Cillian. Are you ready for your surgery?' he asked, picking apart a cheese sandwich.

Right then was the moment I should have seen the red flags. I'd done my reading on Dr. White and thought his name was Tony. However, buried somewhere in the back of my extremely anxious brain, I remember seeing the name Cillian on the profile website. I sort of waved it off because there could have been a number of explanations, and the team at this clinic had already gone above and beyond to put me at ease. I figured I was probably remembering things wrong, then dismissed it. Besides, they already had my money.

There was no going back now.

I nodded, standing there with my bottled water in hand and trying to get away because I was too shy to talk to the gorgeous surgeon. Then, when it went silent, I stumbled to fill the void. 'The team are really sweet and caring. They ran me through everything that's going to happen, taking extra time to assure me everything is going to be okay.'

'Ah, you're one of the nervous ones.'

'Are there many of us?'

The surgeon – Cillian, although now we know

that's utter bullshit and that he absolutely was *not* a surgeon of any kind – shrugged and popped some grated cheddar into his mouth. 'Everyone is nervous on one level or another. Some more than others. But honestly, it will be fine. You'll breathe through the mask, have the best sleep of your life, then wake up and be taken back to your room for some food.'

I thanked Cillian and then went to sit by the window. There were very few people to actually watch in this sleepy little town, but that didn't stop me from trying. I studied them as they went past, but something else kept stealing my attention.

Sometimes, things just feel a little off. That was what I was experiencing right then, but I found myself making excuses for the inconsistencies. The team were so downright impressive with their approach to customer care that it would have been unfair to judge them based on my own insecurities. The simple fact was that a surgeon was recommended, I'd had a Zoom call to discuss the operation, and then they'd made every effort to make me feel comfortable.

Was I entirely happy that the first time I met Dr. White was in the cafeteria while he devoured a sandwich? Well... I was still trying to figure out if I cared or if the alarm bells in my head were just nerves trying to protect me. I decided on the latter and tried to relax, but my body was riddled with prickly anxiety while I waited to be called up.

It wouldn't be long now, I told myself. Not long, and I'd look completely different.

Naturally, I began to fantasise about my new life. Freddy wouldn't recognise me, strangers would treat me differently because I'd be significantly easier on the eye, and – best of all – I'd no longer have to see that murdering bitch every time I looked in a mirror.

No wonder I overlooked the red flags.

I was desperate.

Thinking back, I never did see anything that connected Cillian to the surgery itself. I didn't see him in the theatre at all, and nor did he talk to me in the clinic about the aftercare. I should have put it together right then that there was a reason his name sounded familiar.

Tony White's bio mentioned his son.

I just hadn't thought it through.

In fact, Tony's name completely sank into the

background of my brain. There was so much going on in my life that I didn't have space or time to process all the details about that. Anyway, my face was as sore as a smacked arse after all that surgery. The compression garment made it so I couldn't breathe, and the plaster over my nose wasn't helping. I wanted to just go home and lie down (on my back, as that was all that was allowed), then sleep until everything was fully healed. It doesn't sound like much trouble, but it was a living hell.

Just not compared to what was around the corner for me.

Out in the clinic's car park, abandoned like an unwanted puppy, I waited for my cousin. Time dragged on and on, my worry that something had happened to her growing deeper by the minute. That's when Cillian stepped in to save the day. I never did hear from Lily again, but at least I had somewhere to stay for the foreseeable future.

What came next is particularly interesting to me now.

When Cillian showed me around the magnificent house in which I would be staying, my eyes went straight to the pictures on the walls. My brain chewed up the information and spat it out, almost as if it didn't *want* to acknowledge the truth. Most of the photos were of Cillian, and nobody is vain enough to hang photos of themselves (with the exception of David Hasselhoff). It should have been obvious that these photos were owned by a different man – a man who's proud of his son.

A plastic surgeon.

A *real* plastic surgeon.

But there was something else, too. The more I saw of the property, the less likely it seemed that Cillian had earned this place by himself. Taking a shot in the dark, I guessed he was around my age – mid-thirties or thereabouts – and after years of medical school, there was hardly any time to gain a fortune so big that it could afford him a place like this.

Once again, however, ignorance was bliss.

I convinced myself he'd inherited some money.

It never occurred to me that I should ask about his father.

Like an idiot, I took all that information and simply tossed it aside. I neglected the red flags caused by the barred windows and Cillian's short fuse. My freedom had been taken from me long before I even realised it. All that remained was my complete trust in this man who had got me through such extreme plastic surgery, helping me out by taking care of me when nobody else would. I suppose it felt like I owed him something, which held me back when it came to my pitiful escape attempts. It's like I didn't want to leave at all.

But trust me... I did.

I *really* did.

Chapter 26
Freddy, Now

I HAVE no idea where the other man came from, but he's left the door open and given me a chance. Let me tell you, I'm far beyond wanting to call the police, and this surgeon friend of Daisy's is not going to stand in the way of my revenge.

That bitch killed my brother.

It's only fair that I kill her.

The door is only slightly ajar, but I run towards it quickly. There's a voice on the other side. A man's voice, deep and frustrated as he tells someone it's his house and he can be there whenever he likes. That's when I stand to one side, just to get my bearings.

Because there's a fight coming.

Now, look, I'm a big guy. Fighting always came

naturally to me, and for some reason, I always found it more exciting than scary. But taking on two people is a little on the risky side. The man who's just arrived is old – his heart might give in if I burst in quick enough – but the younger man looks fit and healthy. Not only that, but there's a certain confidence in the way he carries himself. I noticed it from upon the hill, and if it's that obvious from afar...

It doesn't matter. They might be protecting Daisy – I don't care – and she needs to get what's coming to her. It doesn't matter what your excuse is, you can't just kill a man and leave town, then not expect his family to make you pay for what you did.

And Daisy? She'll pay.

She'll pay big time.

Chapter 27
Daisy, Now

Iᴛ's hard to say how long I've been down here, but it's not getting any easier.

Although my mouth is stone dry and my stomach is starting to grumble like a dying motor, it can't have been more than a few hours since I woke up. There is a very small window the size of a letter box right at the top of the wall, and it's just big enough to see the sun setting through the thick blades of grass that obscure my view. It's the only way for me to measure time, which offers at least a little comfort.

Then again, who am I kidding?

It's not like I'll ever see the sun again.

The idea haunts me. Taunts me. A strange,

hollowing sensation carves out my stomach. I wrap my arms around it, shake my head to try staying awake while fatigue hits me out of nowhere. It's all that stress and adrenaline. It's exhausting, and I want to sleep.

But there are more worthwhile things to do.

Like get the hell out of here.

It might be a pathetically naïve thought, but I've seen films where people use a hairpin to pick a lock. Don't ask me how they do it, but when I feel around the top of my head, I'm overwhelmed with relief to find I have one available. I pull it out and start to creep up the creaky wooden stairs, then drop to my knees and try playing around with the concept. I have no idea how this is done or what the inside of a lock looks like, but it's worth a try...

Isn't it?

After five minutes or so of invading the lock with the hairpin, hope is starting to become a stranger. I drop it to the floor, giving up with a sigh. My back rests against the wall, one foot on the stairs and the other pushing between the railings of the banister. It's then that I start thinking about Cillian and how stupid I was to come home with him. My parents always used to tell me not to trust strangers. I should have listened. I should have trusted my instincts.

While I wallow in self-pity, I start to hear a muffled conversation. Sitting up, I press my ear to the door and find it's more than that. It's a ruckus. There are two voices. Maybe even three – it's hard to tell if the third is a different person or a change in tone.

But one of them is definitely Cillian.

I would recognise that furious yelling anywhere.

'Stay the hell away from that cellar, you bastard!'

My head jerks back in shock. That deep, angry tone always scared the life out of me, and this is no different. But who is he talking to? Whose footprints are stomping down the hall? I sit up, my heart fluttering. The lock turns. *Clunk.* A smile spreads across my face as I picture Tony White taking me into town. Liberating me.

Saving my life.

The door whines as the handle turns down. The basement light comes on behind me, flooding the room. The door opens widely but, somehow, almost in slow motion. Hope seizes me, but I feel my smile vanish as the door opens farther. Then I realise with horror that Tony's face is not Tony's face at all. It's a flash from the past – a demon I've been trying to evade. But now, while this man towers over me with nothing but raw hate in his eyes, it's abundantly clear that I'm done running. After all this time, he's finally caught up to me – Freddy has found me, and I'm right where I should be.

On my knees.

THE REST of the chaos happens in an instant.

Freddy reaches out to grab my shirt, but he misses as I back away. My footing is poor, and I slip, but only enough to knock me down a step. By then, the shadow comes rushing up the hall behind Freddy. Cillian appears behind my brother-in-law, and suddenly, I realise just how big he really is – Freddy has always been tall, but my captor towers above even him.

My body goes cold at the very first sight of him. I open my mouth to scream, but only a weak, pathetic breath comes out like a wheeze. Freddy turns and reaches for Cillian's throat. The two of them wrestle like that while I freeze, wondering if I could rush past them and into the hall. But there's no way – they're filling up the space as they violently attack each other in a hail of grunts and ferocious, guttural roars.

Petrified that I might get caught in the middle of this, I come to my senses and back all the way down the stairs. It's just as well I did because Cillian then overpowers Freddy and shoves him hard enough to make him tumble down after me. There's banging and crashing as Freddy rolls down to the bottom. I gasp, staring up at Cillian, who smirks for only an instant before turning his back on me to speak with somebody in the hall. Tony, probably. Then, just as he always will, he shuts the door.

And locks it again.

What happens next is as confusing to me as it would be to an outsider. I rush forward and drop to my knees, my trembling hands feeling around Freddy's chest to see if he's breathing. I'm praying the fall didn't kill him, just so I won't be alone down here, dying in complete solitude. But I feel nothing. No breath. No sign of life at all.

Until he groans and wriggles.

'Freddy,' I say in a breath of relief, helping him to his feet.

While he gets up, his eyes wander around the room. My brother-in-law, who has hunted me this entire time, studies his surroundings with growing horror, one hand rubbing the back of his head, which must have taken some knocks on his way down the stairs. I stand up with him, aiding him as he tries to adjust to his cell... or his final resting place.

Then his eyes find me.

It's hard to describe the horror of the way he looks at me. It's like he's been pushed to his limits. As his cheeks turn red and his eyes widen, his jaw tightens. It looks like a volcano that's about to erupt, and all I can do is try to settle him.

'It's okay,' I say nervously. 'We're down here together, but we'll get out if we just—'

That's when his hand lashes out like a whip. It wraps around my throat, where a short gargling sound breaks loose. Freddy stands up taller, then puts his other hand around my neck. My own hands rush up, trying desperately to pull the fingers away and loosen the grip. But he's too strong. He was *always* too strong.

'Listen to me,' I try to say, but I don't even know if the words leave my lips.

Freddy's eyes bore into me as he continues to

squeeze. Harder. Harder still. My throat is in agony, and my lungs demand air that they're simply not going to get. My face becomes hot, and my eyes start to grow heavy. All I can think of is that this must be what dying feels like.

This must be how Jason felt when he took his last breath.

Perhaps I deserve this. It could be that I'm finally getting my comeuppance. As Freddy's grip tightens and my vision starts to blur, I at least get to experience one moment of clarity and peace, knowing that it could have been a lot worse.

At least I don't have to stay with Cillian any more.

THE MOMENT he lets go of my throat, regret burns in his eyes.

I gasp for breath, lightly touching my neck as if it will help me somehow, while Freddy grits his teeth, clenches a fist, then fights every temptation to punish me for what I did to his brother. Then it occurs to me he doesn't know Jason was a bully. Not that it will change things.

'Thank...' the wheezing allows me to say, '... you.'

'For what? Not squeezing the life out of you?' Freddy flaps a hand like he's done with me, then has a walk around the cellar like I did only minutes ago. When he realises there's nowhere else to go, he stops in front of me where I now sit on the stairs to recover. 'Just so we're clear, the only reason you're still breathing is because I might need your help getting out of here. You *are* going to die because I know you killed my brother.'

I didn't need the cold, stinking reminder, and once again, I feel nothing but shame. Naturally, my brain rebels and tries to justify my actions, but there's just no excusing murder. Maybe when I'm out of here, I'll learn to hate myself as much as Freddy hates me.

'You look different.'

'Thanks.'

'I wasn't complimenting you.'

'How did you know about Jason?' I ask, the burn in my throat easing off.

'Does it matter?'

'Just curious.'

Freddy shakes his head at me in disbelief, then goes to sit on the far side of the cellar... on the floor.

It's obvious he's keeping his distance so he doesn't do anything stupid. His restraint is actually admirable. 'After I saw you that night, I headed back in the direction you came from and saw tyre tracks in the mud outside the woods. I went in, poked around a little, then found some unearthed soil. My shovel was in the Jeep from my day at work, so I got digging and found...'

It's hard for him to say, which is completely understandable. I look him in the eye.

'I'm so sorry.'

'He was my brother.'

'My husband.'

'Just tell me why.'

'It was self-defence.' There's too long a silence, so I add, 'It got out of hand.'

While Freddy sits with his face buried in his hands, I tell him everything. About what happened with Jason that night. About how close he'd come to finding me when I went on the run. About Cillian, the way he's treated me, and what he intends to do with me now. Well, with *us*. Freddy's shoulders bob up and down as the details emerge. Then he looks up, and for the first time ever, there are tears glistening in his eyes.

'For what it's worth,' he says, wiping them

away with his sleeve, 'I'm sorry you've gone through all of this. That doesn't mean I forgive you – I still have every intention of getting my revenge as soon as we're out of here – but the situation is complicated... and I understand.'

I try not to let the threat bother me because my current choices are to either die down here or help Freddy get out and then die having done something good for once. It's not the most settling thought, but it's something. First, though, I want to know something.

'How did you know I was down here?'

'I didn't.'

'Then how did you find me?'

'That man – Cillian, I think you said – told me not to go to the cellar. Of course, I came right here. I just wasn't aware of what he was like. I actually thought he was sheltering you. *Protecting* you. Guess he's done a good job of covering things up.'

My head is nodding of its own volition. I think back to Manuel and Isabella. How they've paid the price just so Cillian could keep me here. My memory flies back to the times I've tried escaping and how hard it's been. Could it be that having Freddy here would benefit me? Will his brains and strength be useful when we work together to get out? What about Tony – will he see his son for the monster he really is and help us, or is psychosis a genetic trait?

There's only one way to find out, and that's by starting with one question.

I look Freddy dead in the eye and ask.

'What do we do?'

Chapter 28
Daisy, Now

'There's no way that will work,' I say, shaking my head.

In reality, there might be a chance. I just don't want to believe that it could be that simple because if hope is torn away from me once more, I don't think I'll survive. There have been too many opportunities. There have been just as many failures.

'We need to give it a chance,' Freddy tells me, pacing back and forth while I sit at the base of the stairs, wringing my hands. 'I don't like this any more than you do – believe me, the last thing on my mind is touching you – but if this Cillian fella is as much of a creep as you say, we need to take advantage of that. No matter how much it makes me shiver.'

'You know we'll only get one chance at this?'

'Right, of course. That's why it has to work.'

'We could just... wait it out.'

'That could be hours or days, and even then, they could just be coming to kill us.'

I hate to admit it, but he's right. This has to be the dumbest plan, but it's sure as hell better than no plan at all. My brain gives it a once-over just to make sure there's nothing else, and then it's time to give Freddy a nod. To give him permission to try this out.

He begins by kneeling in front of me. I open my legs and let him come close to me. Even before everything that's happened, it still would have made me shiver to come anywhere near Freddy. It's not that he's unattractive – you could argue that he's even better looking than Jason was, with a good tan and some muscles that are hopefully as good for function as they are for fashion. The thing is, like it or not, this is my brother-in-law.

Not that Cillian knows it.

'Are you ready?' he asks, inches from my mouth and desperately avoiding eye contact.

I don't answer. I just open my mouth to let out a moan of pleasure. Freddy hasn't touched me, not even a little bit, as this is all for show. A performance. For display purposes only. He keeps an eye over my shoulder as I lean back on the stairs, the sharp, wooden steps jutting into my spine. It's painful but nowhere near as painful as the idea of staying here forever.

Another moan escapes my lips. Louder and longer this time. I feel like an idiot – like one of those porn stars faking an orgasm with all the acting talent of Emma Watson (I always hated her). We both look up at the door, waiting, hoping, but not realistically expecting...

'Nothing,' I say.

'You'll have to go louder.'

'I feel so dumb.'

'Just shut up and moan.'

'I can't do both.'

'This is no time for—'

The door swings open. In an instant, Freddy's hands are all over me. I continue to make sounds like a woman being pleasured, arcing my back as Freddy thrusts into me. Nothing is actually going in, I hasten to remind you, but it's hard for the peeping Tom to tell, given our position on the stairs. Aiming to make him jealous enough that he'll come close, I lean back and glare at the top of the stairs with a sly, provoking smile.

But it's not Cillian staring down at us.

It's his father.

'No,' he says, and this is the first time I've clearly heard his voice. The old man shakes his head, reaches for something that looks like a crowbar, then starts pounding down the stairs towards us. 'Hey, break that up. Do you have any idea what Cillian will do if he sees this?'

We don't listen. Tony needs to come closer. Freddy carries on as if he hasn't even noticed we have an audience, but I feel his knee shift. That's him putting his foot in a position to spring up, I think, and then I finally look him in the eye as the footsteps come closer...

Closer...

And then it's time.

———————

THE NEXT THING I see is Freddy's hand shooting out, reaching.

Tony screams at the top of his lungs, but it's not from the grab. It's at the same crashing sound that slams against the stairs behind me. Something hard hits the back of my head – a knee, perhaps – and then Freddy leaps over me to pull him down.

He grabs the crowbar and hurls it across the room, disarming him. Before I know it, I'm caught in a tangle between the two. None of us can move. Freddy's cheeks are red with rage, and I can only hear Tony whining like the old man he is above me.

'Please,' he says. 'I'm no fighter. I only want to look out for you.'

My heart bleeds. Truly, it does. I look to Freddy, who stares at me with the same vacant expression I must be giving off. We must both be deep in thought with the same thing going on in our heads: is this man anywhere near as bad as his son?

In the silence, I crane my neck to look up at the door. It's still wide open. That's our opportunity. Then I look at Freddy again. He nods, telling me to leave while I still can. Contorting multiple parts of my body throbbing in hot pain, I squeeze my way out from between the two, find my way to my feet, and look back at them both.

Tony looks old. Older than his pictures by about five years and harmless. The lower lip quivers in his white beard as he lies on his back at the bottom few feet of the stairs. Freddy has his weight on him, a clenched fist raised and ready to strike, only holding the pose long enough for me to squeeze past him... if I dare trust the old man.

'Go,' Freddy says. 'Quit wasting time.'

Without a word, my gaze falls upon the open door at the top of the stairs. This chance isn't going to come again, so I snap out of my fear and begin my ascent, stepping over Tony and hurrying upwards as fast as I can, excitement jolting through me as I finally escape the—

Something hard around my ankle. Fierce. It yanks, hard. I lose my footing as the stairs rush up at my face. Somehow, I protect myself with my arms, but one of them catches a hangnail. Blood spits and then trickles. I ignore it, kick my clamped foot wildly, and then the grip releases. Dripping with sweat, I quickly turn back to find Tony being dragged down the last of the stairs. Freddy moves to wrestle with him, but Tony displays unusual strength and manages to pin him against the cellar wall. I hesitate. For too long.

'What are you waiting for?' my brother-in-law screams. 'Run!'

It's a hard thing to do, but somehow, I finally manage to follow the simple instruction. I turn and dash up the stairs, which suddenly feel ten times longer than ever before. The door up above is wide open, beckoning me, promising freedom. I keep expecting Cillian to step into the doorway – 'Gotcha!' he might yell with a menacing cackle – but it doesn't happen.

Somehow, I make it upstairs.

Only I've lost all sense of direction. It feels like months since I last came up here, but it can't have been more than a day. I stop in the hall and look up both ends, only vaguely aware of the commotion in the cellar. The hallway lights feel blindingly bright, and I squint, panting heavily, confused as to where I am. Is this the effect of my head trauma, I wonder? Or Freddy squeezing my throat so hard that I almost died?

It doesn't matter. It's time to go.

I pick a direction and run, ending up in the kitchen. So many memories took place here, none of them good. This room is linked to the main hall – I remember that much – but somehow, I can't figure out which door leads there. It's the panic. It must be. But then, an older memory resurfaces. One of Cillian showing me around the house and the route he took.

Suddenly, I remember a different route.

The living room... with the glass wall.

Feeling lighter than air with the promise of

freedom, I start to run again, zooming through the kitchen towards the door. My liberation is so close I can almost taste it. I'll send for help – get Freddy out of the cellar and pray it's not too late. All good intentions. All good odds.

Until a hulking figure barrels into me.

And knocks me to the floor.

THE HARD TILES rush up to greet me.

This time, my arms can't move fast enough. My chin takes the fall. My *healing* chin. At least it was. I cry out as pain sears up my jawline, and then I roll on to my back and look my attacker in the eye. I already know who it is before I see him.

It's Cillian.

And he's smiling.

Tears stinging my eyes, I roll over again and start crawling away, my feet slipping out from under me each time I try to get up. Cillian's laugh sounds from behind me, cruel and mocking. Like he never cared about me at all. Like I was only ever an object of entertainment.

No surprise there.

'You really think you can get away from me?'

he says with dull humour in his voice. His shadow slowly takes a step every time I move, following me. He's never going to let me go. 'Even if you get out of here, you'll have to get into town. Good luck with that, Daisy. I have a car. Weapons. Strength. What do you have? An inferiority complex and a whiny voice?'

I shake off the comments like they can never hurt me. Determination carries me across the floor. One hand in front of the other, my breath desperate and hurried. I'm picking up speed now, getting closer and closer to the door until it feels like I'm gliding. Weightless.

Then I realise in a heartbeat.

Cillian has lifted me off the floor.

As soon as I'm on my feet, he hurls me against the oven. My knee smacks against the door, and I scream. Trying to stand up, Cillian intercepts me and shoves me back, the heels of his hands knocking the wind from my lungs. It doesn't take long to spot the knife. I hesitate before reaching, quickly recognising this situation is an exact repeat of what ruined my life.

That extra second is all he needs to stop me.

His hand swats mine away, and then he pushes me again. I reach for something to hold on to, grab something hard, and then it comes down with me. Nothing fixed. A glass bottle that smashes against the floor tiles when it lands. Something acidic quickly filling the air. I'd know that smell anywhere because Jason always made me use it.

Cooking oil.

It's no use trying to get up. My hands slide on the oil, sending me straight back to the floor. Cillian laughs once more, then reaches for my shirt. I'm in the air again, held up by his monstrous strength as I try to slap him and push him away, but the oil makes my hand slip off. It's like trying to hurt someone who can't be hurt.

All the while, he laughs.

Always laughing.

My eyes roam the dimly lit kitchen, my feet kicking and thrashing around while I look for something – anything – I can use to get me out. It's no use. Cillian has me in his grasp, and he'll never let me go. Even if he'd ever intended to, that chance vanished when I decided to run. When Freddy came in to get me... or to kill me. Where is he now?

I barely get a chance to wonder before Cillian throws me again. This time, my body slams into the dining table. Something bright and hot rolls past

me, and I quickly pull my hand away. An instanta-
neous reaction. One I'm grateful for. Because as it
rolls off the table and hits the floor, time finally
slows down enough for me to see what it was.

It was a candle.

And it kisses the oil on the floor.

The rest is one bright, fiery blur.

Chapter 29
Daisy, Then

I WAS afraid killing might not have been a one-time thing.

After what I'd done to Jason, there was no doubting this side of myself existed, but was it still there within me somewhere? Was my ability to murder another human being now a permanent resident in my subconscious? I only ask because I wanted it.

I wanted to kill Cillian.

It was a gruesome, ugly thought, but I couldn't stop it. Even on that late Tuesday (I think) night, locked away in the bedroom and cuddling my pillow on the bed, all I could think about was seeing my captor's face turn from smug to lifeless in a short space of time. The idea that I might cause something like that was scarily exciting. The only thing was, I didn't know if it was a means of escape or because I might have enjoyed it.

The very thought of that made my blood run cold.

Thankfully, there was an interruption to these dark, intrusive considerations: a slight rap on the door, the turning of a key from the outside, and Cillian's face appearing in the gap of the doorway. All within five seconds, and no other warning.

It was like he'd hoped to catch me off guard.

Or to see more than I would have wanted him to.

'Good evening, Daisy,' he said without coming in. 'I just wanted to swing by and make sure every-thing is okay. Locking you in here certainly isn't ideal, but you understand why it was necessary, no? It's for your own protection.'

At this stage of my incarceration, he hadn't even tried to kiss me yet. The incident by the pool had not yet happened. It was extremely confusing why he might think I needed protection, but there was a childlike cruelness in his eyes – they'd turned beady rather than their usual beautiful sapphire. It was like he wasn't seeing me. Not *really* seeing me.

'I understand' was all I thought to say.

'Do you though? Because you look upset.'

'Not upset. It just gets...' I stopped myself from saying 'lonely' as he probably would have used that as an excuse to keep me company. Pivoting, I finished the sentence in a way to avoid that. 'Frustrating with how tired I get. All I want is to sleep.'

Cillian nods, mouth open, almost untrusting. 'Yes, your body is working hard to heal from all the surgery. It takes more energy, you understand, so it's perfectly normal to feel drained. Just rest as much as possible. I'm around the house somewhere. I'm *always* around.'

With that, the door closed. The lock turned again. It was a deep, hideous metallic sound that reminded me of a prison cell. A shiver ran through me, so I got under the duvet and turned off the light. There was no chance whatsoever of getting out of there that night – if at all – so I just lay in the foetal position and let my might wander.

I expected to sleep, but all that came back to me were those thoughts. What if I couldn't find a way out of here? Did Cillian have to die? I suffered the prolonged, haunting sensation of actually *wanting* to do it, but could I even go through with it again? I remembered how it felt the first time – the panic, the flustering worry, the extreme and torturing guilt of having taken a man's hopes and dreams. Even his potential for the future. All gone.

Because of me.

But among all of this, I couldn't stop thinking about how much Cillian was actually doing the same thing to me. It wasn't that he was actually trying to kill me, but the old me was dying. If I ever got out of there, how much of the original Daisy would be left? Not much, I bet, so I stayed awake long into the early hours wondering that if I did go through with it, how would I do it? I didn't think I could stab someone again. Not after Jason.

I would have to find another way.

You KNOW the rest of the story already, but there's a little more to tell.

Over the coming days, it was important that I tried to appear happy – to hide my disdain from Cillian just to keep him calm. In the meantime, I rested and relaxed as much as possible, burying my head in book after book. It was a nightmare trying to concentrate, my attention constantly wandering as the concept of murder emerged time after time.

One day, when Cillian had vanished somewhere in the house as he usually did, it occurred to me that there *was* a way to kill him. Even if I decided not to use it, the option was right there. It would just take a little research and preparation. Maybe a daring risk, if I had the balls. I closed the book I was reading and carried it upstairs towards the library, pausing only when Cillian appeared in his bedroom doorway, a toothbrush hanging from his mouth. When he saw me, he stared at me, removed the toothbrush, then pointed it at the book in my hand.

'Are you done with another one?'

'I'm giving up on this one.'

'Not to your taste?'

'Just getting a little tired of fiction.'

'Not much non-fiction here, I'm afraid. Except for medical textbooks.'

I nodded slowly. 'May I peruse those shelves?'

'Be my guest, but you'll find them boring.'

'It'll just be a nice change.'

Cillian disappeared back into the bedroom, heading for the en suite. I remember walking past feeling joyous and uplifted, the possibility of escape finally re-emerging. See, I wanted to create a poison but had no idea how to do it. The only way to learn was to use one of those books, but how was I supposed to hide what I was reading from him? Now that he knew what I was doing – without the real reason behind it, that is – I felt like there was more freedom.

It was one less thing to hide.

It took days to figure out how this would work. As it turned out, medicine was not such a straight-forward thing. I spent so much time in the study, in my bed, lounging around in the living room and burying my head in book after book after book. I was desperate to find a cure for my imprisonment, and it was beginning to appear completely impossible.

Until I read about a particular ingredient.

Oleander.

My heart raced as I read the word over and over. I remembered Cillian pointing to the pretty pink flower on the windowsill in the utility room. It was a gift from his friends in California, he'd told me, and then warned me not to touch it as it may cause a highly unpleasant rash. Now, as I leafed through the next few pages as if to spoil the ending for myself, I devoured the information about how mixing it with certain household chemicals may give it an extremely high chance of causing death.

That word – *death* – leapt off the page and held my attention.

All of it.

But it wasn't a guarantee it would work. I wasn't even certain I could summon the courage to poison Cillian, but it was good to know how. I memorised the concoction, thankfully realising it wasn't too complicated, and spent the next few days noting where the rest of the ingredients were. It was important that I made it easy for myself, learning the location of all the ingredients so it would be fast and easy to make the poison if I could bring myself to do it.

Although, again, there was no guarantee it would work.

For the next few nights, I had horrendous dreams about slipping some of the cocktail into his food. Cillian's eyes bulged as he scratched at his own throat, dropping to the ground and writhing in pain while his insides burned. In some of these dreams, he got back up and knew what I'd done to him, then punished me in multiple ways. I frequently woke up in cold sweats, no longer wanting to be his prisoner – realising the hard way that a backup plan was vital to this operation if I wanted to protect myself.

That was when I decided for absolute certain: I would make the poison and keep it nearby, just in case I magically became brave enough to use it or if the opportunity presented itself. But life was built on options, and I wanted a backup plan. I wanted to feel safe.

That's why I still considered the knife.

IT TOOK me a couple of days to make the poison. A little bit of stealing here, some almost getting caught there. Each time Cillian had his back turned, I gathered one additional ingredient after the other until I was finally able to mix it all. As for where to put it? Well, you would think Cillian had some medical vials lying around. He did, but I had to work crazy hard to find them.

After the day where he flipped out on me for eyeing up Chris Pratt, I knew extra precautions were necessary. I had gone from feeling unsafe to feeling clearly and obviously in immediate danger. A potentially non- or slow-acting poison wasn't going to cut it, so I took a kitchen knife from the drawer – it would have been harder to notice that than one missing from the knife block – and hid it under my mattress with the vial. I only got halfway up the stairs with it before realising just how bad an idea that really was.

Scissors, I thought. *You should take scissors. That would be much easier to explain.*

Not that I intended to be caught, but it was the safer play. I returned quickly and replaced the knife with scissors, then hurried to my room and placed them under my mattress, beside the poison. As soon as that was done, I leaned into the hallway to see if Cillian had seen me, blew out a quick sigh of relief, then closed the door.

Then my heart sank.

'What are we hiding, Daisy?'

I gasped and spun around. Cillian was sitting there in the bedroom chair, one leg resting over the other, his hands interwoven and resting comfortably on his stomach. I felt hot and anxious, like a teacher had caught me doing something wrong. Something *very* wrong.

'Nothing,' I stuttered. 'It... I...'

'You wouldn't happen to be stealing from me, would you?'

'No! It's not that. It's... I mean...'

Shaking his head with disappointment, Cillian rose from the chair and slowly crossed the room. I shrank back as he passed me, but his eyes weren't on me – they were focused on the bed. When he lifted the mattress, I was so tempted to turn and run for my life. The only reason I didn't was because I probably wouldn't have made it, but I'd have looked more guilty.

Cillian stared under the mattress, sighed audibly, and cleared his throat.

'What exactly did you plan to use these for?' he asked.

'It's...' My brain failed me. 'Nothing.'

'They serve no purpose whatsoever?'

I shook my head, then realised he couldn't see me. In the silence, he then reached for the hidden items, dropped the mattress, and turned to face me. Now, it's hard to explain why I could feel so positive in a situation like this, but when I saw that he'd only found the scissors – *not* the poison – I could have laughed right in his face.

This would be easy to get around.

'I was thinking about trimming my hair,' I said. 'That's all.'

'Hmm. And you didn't think to ask me?'

'You seemed stressed, and you've already done so much for me.'

'That's...' Cillian lowered his eyes. 'Actually rather considerate.'

Relief huffed out of my lips... quietly. 'Sorry, I should have asked.'

'That's okay. I'll sort out a haircut for you before you leave. But no scissors, okay?'

'Okay.'

'You promise you won't try this again?'

'I promise.'

'Good.'

Cillian left the room, taking the scissors with him. As soon as the door was shut again, I rushed to the mattress and almost tossed it off the bed. The poison was gone, but where? There's no way Cillian would have seen that and left me unpunished. I dropped to my knees and felt around, squeezing my arm between the thin gap in the bed slats. When my fingers finally touched the vial, I snatched it up and returned it to my pocket, thanking any and all gods for letting me get away with creating a vial of murder fluid.

It was going to stay with me from now on. At all times.

Because who knew when I would need it the most?

Chapter 30
Daisy, Now

THE BLAZE SPREADS across the kitchen, the floor lighting up like a runway strip towards the oven. The previously dim room now glows hot orange and yellow, flickering and flashing while I drop to my knees, exhausted. It takes only a few seconds before Cillian is on me.

'Look what you've done now!' he screams above the crackle and hiss. Then, through a clenched jaw, he spits, 'All you had to do was sit there and look pretty. Dad's team made that possible, so there was literally nothing to do but what you were told. You could have had everything. This house. My affection. All great things that others would die for!'

The terror is setting in now. I try getting up

from my knees, but Cillian's firm hand locks on to my shoulder and holds me down. Never in my life have I regretted anything more than letting him see me hide the scissors. How useful those would be in this situation. All I have now is this stupid vial of worthless poison in my pocket.

It's not enough to defend myself.

'Say something,' Cillian yells, pinching deeply into my shoulder. '*Say something!*'

Some words spring to mind. Harsh ones. But they don't leave my lips. The truth is, I'm too scared to say anything at all. This is the second time I've faced death in the kitchen with a big, scary man standing over me.

It makes me wonder, if I had the knife, could I do it?

Cillian loses any restraint he still had, using both hands to shove me. I pivot and fall on to my stomach. I'm near the door again, desperately crawling towards it while the flames spread. Fire is supposed to be hot, but it's making me slick with sweat, even from the other side of the kitchen. I feel the damp between my palms and the kitchen tiles. My top clings to my chest. Cillian's shadow reaches over me as I close the distance between myself and the door.

I'm not getting out of here.

It's obvious.

Then, as if to prove my point, Cillian leans down and seizes my arm. His hand is like a horse's mouth, engulfing my bicep in a vice-like grip. There, he flips me on to my back and stands with a leg to either side of me. The flickering embers cast a dark shadow over his features. He was always a demon on the inside, but now he actually looks like one.

'Say it,' he demands. 'Just say it.'

'Say what?' My hands raise to my face like they can protect me.

They can't.

'Tell me you love me,' he says now, his hands shaking as something white glistens on his cheek. It's not until the light catches it that I realise it's a tear. 'Tell me you're better than my mother. Tell me there's at least one woman on this earth capable of loving me.'

It suddenly sinks in that there's much more to this than just psychosis. Cillian has suffered neglect. From the looks of it, his earliest introduction to women – his mother – left him bitter as well as a lunatic. No wonder he wanted to keep me... he longs to be loved.

If only he had gone about it the right way.

'No,' I tell him. 'I could have loved you. You had all the makings of a good man.'

Cillian gasps, but I continue ruthlessly, tasting every drop of hate.

'You had a nice home, good looks, and you even had me thinking you were a career man. Not only was none of it true, but you're a bully. You're domineering and mean. You have no control over your own actions. You're like a child.'

'Shut up!'

'See? You're lashing out. All I want to do is leave.'

'You'll tell the police!'

'Damn right I will. Don't you think I should?'

In the longest pause this world has ever known, Cillian stops to think. His fists unclench, elongating as the fire grows closer. Hotter. He seems to notice this, crooking his head to one side, then looks around the room. When he finds what he wants, he takes two short steps and pulls the fire extinguisher off the wall. It won't be enough to douse the flames.

But that's not what he wants it for.

'I'll never let you go,' he says. 'You'll always be here... but only in my memory.'

It doesn't immediately register what he means, but it soon makes sense. When he lifts the extinguisher high above his head – high above *my* head – more glowing tears streak down his cheeks. It's just me and him in that moment. The final moment of my life.

The last thing I hear is his frenzied scream.

The last thing I see is him bringing the extinguisher down on me.

———

It's NOT the blow of the extinguisher that I hear. There is something hard and clunking – a strike hard enough to freeze time. I stare up at Cillian through slitted eyes, half wanting to hide from the incoming attack, half wanting to see what just happened.

Mostly, I want to see.

Cillian lingers for a moment, then drops the extinguisher on the floor beside me. I shriek, then scoot back against the wall as my attacker drops to his knees. There he stays for only a second or two before his body slumps to the floor, eyes and mouth equally wide.

Then Freddy steps into view, crowbar in hand.

Only he's not here to save me.

Because his hate has turned on me.

'Please,' I whimper. 'Please let me go. I'll do anything.'

Freddy steps forward and then gets down on his haunches, the crowbar clenched tight in his fist. The look in his eye is nothing like the one of well-acted passion down in the cellar. There's no lust there. There's not even toleration. It's just pure, unbridled hate.

'What about bringing my brother back to life? Would you do that?'

'You... You know I can't.'

'Then what good are you?'

'I can help you out of here.'

'Look around you, Daisy. Does it seem like I need help?'

Across the room, something explodes. We both cover our faces, my heart almost bursting from my chest. When I look up, it's the microwave that's blown into pieces. The flames have swallowed it just like they have with most of the kitchen. Now, the beams are charring as the embers scale them like monkeys up a tree.

Freddy turns back to me. 'This is nothing like the hell you'll be burning in.'

'I didn't want to kill him,' I whine. 'He was my husband. I loved him.'

'Then why did you do it?'

'Because he was attacking me!'

'And then what? You thought you'd just bury him in the woods like some animal? I grew up with that man, you little bitch. We have over thirty years of memories together. We built forts, we fought, we helped each other get women back when they weren't killers. That's all gone now. It's all gone because of you, and you can't even take any bloody responsibility for it! Try telling me I'm wrong. I dare you.'

My gaze lowers to the crowbar again. His hand twitches like he's about to swing for me. Meanwhile, the intense heat from the fire is growing closer. The smoke makes its first entry into my lungs, which makes me cough. Freddy's cough shortly follows.

'I'm so, so sorry' is all that's left to say, although I say it without even trying to hide my urgency. If we don't get out of here soon, we'll both die. 'It wasn't like I sat around plotting to kill him. Jason was a bully, and he ran me down every time we spoke. He had a drink problem, and it got him angry. The man I loved was disappearing, so—'

'So you thought you'd kill him?'

'It wasn't like that, but... you're right. I messed up.' The words hit me so hard, the accountability striking me with a new kind of pain. But the taste is... comfortable. The rest speaks for itself. 'The first thing I should have done was call for an ambulance. The police, too. Even though it was a poor reaction on my part, Jason deserved better than to be hidden and forgotten about. I felt so scared, so entitled to my freedom, that I thought of nothing better than to run and change my face. If you'll—'

Another explosion, this time the kettle. It scares the hell out of me so hard that I scream. The flames continue to crackle and pop. Freddy's expression hasn't changed – the whites of his eyes glow as he waits for me to finish my pathetic excuse for murder.

'You have every right to hate me, but if you help me get out of here, then I promise I'll turn myself in to the police. I won't try to run. You have my word. I've done enough running to last a lifetime, and I'm sick of it. It's time to face my past.'

Freddy sighs and rubs his eyes. 'I came here to kill you.'

'You can still do that later if the mood takes you.'

'But you'll try to run.'

'I won't. I promise.'

While my brother-in-law tries to decide whether I have a right to live, the flames start to surround us. My lungs have had enough now, and I start to spew the toxins from the fumes. Freddy joins me, choking and gagging on his own breath while I wait, my entire body aching with tension. Then, he finally looks me in the eye, his expression unreadable.

And says...

Nothing.

Freddy says absolutely nothing, because he's too busy standing up. I panic, swearing blind he's about to leave me to burn alive in this prison. But then he reaches out and grabs my hand, hauling me to my feet with all the strength of his brother. For half a second, it actually feels like Jason again. It's sweetly familiar. Something genetic.

'Thank you,' I tell him, not really knowing what to feel.

Leading me by the hand, he runs through the hallway where he must have come in from earlier on. It's locked, the key missing. Freddy curses, and my own hopes die as fast as Cillian is about to. I look back at the kitchen, where I can still see his feet. I only watch for a second before the flames spread up his leg. There's no movement.

That man is dead now.

It's a weird feeling knowing that a second man has died in a kitchen because of me, but there's no time to worry about it now. All I can think about is the long glass wall in the living room. *Doors*, I remind myself. *They're doors.*

I run for it. Freddy is hot on my trail as the ceiling collapses in the kitchen. A black cloud explodes into the hallway, the smoke turning to grey as it pursues us. Freddy sees the glass immediately and smashes it with the crowbar. Broken glass rains to the floor. Freedom is ours.

The outside gate is wide open. We run towards it together. It's the farthest I've ever got – out of all those escape attempts, I never truly got past the pool. Now, my liberation is right there in front of us. We sprint through it, away from the smouldering building as we leave everything to the fire. Including Cillian. Including...

'Where's Tony?' I ask, stopping in the gateway.

'The old man?' Freddy turns. 'I knocked his arse clean out.'

'You left him to die?'

'It was him or me.'

I hate to admit it, but he's right. He knew we were in the cellar and did nothing to help us get out. But did he deserve to die?

There's no time to think about it. I just want to get away from the fire. Away from the house that broke me down mentally over a number of days or weeks. It doesn't matter that I'll end up in either a cell or a coffin because, after all that's happened, it's about time I stood up and took the blame for what I've done. Jason is dead because of me. Cillian, too, in a weird sort of way. So perhaps what's about to happen is long overdue.

Whatever that is, I deserve it.

Chapter 31
Daisy, Now

WITH THE INFERNO blazing behind us, Freddy and I make it into the field. Thank God the grass isn't too high, or the entire countryside would go up in smoke. I don't even know if there are fire services around here, and even if there is, it would take a while to get here.

Freddy stops ahead, me lagging behind. It's caused a little by the fact that tonight has taken it out of me (emotionally *and* physically), but I'm also scared of this man. It wasn't so long ago that he confessed he'd come here to kill me. That really puts me out of the mood of standing beside him.

By the time I catch up to him, he's gazing beyond me, the fire reflected in his eyes. I turn to follow his line of sight, let out whatever cough remains, and stare back at the mess that used to be the White estate. It's no longer as magnificent as it once was, its wall engulfed in flames, smoke billowing out from its collapsed roof. The far side of it remains intact, however, and that is where the image first makes itself clear.

'Is that...?' Freddy says from behind me.

'Yes. I think so.'

Far ahead, Tony comes stumbling across the grass. He slips, trips, and falls as he makes his way towards us. His voice calls in the distance, and although it's hard to make out what he's saying, the torture in his voice is more than evident. That's when it hits me.

His son just died.

Before I can even begin to process this, Freddy breezes past me, his arms swinging like an ape whose territory has just been invaded. I've seen that walk before – Jason did it whenever he was about to hit someone. Words can't describe how much I hate Tony for being part of what Cillian did to me, but the cycle of hurting people has to end somewhere.

I take off after Freddy, calling his name. He doesn't listen – only storming towards Tony, who has collapsed now and is howling for his dead son.

Freddy doesn't seem to care because he's grabbed the old man by his shirt, his other hand raised in a fist.

'You sick son of a bitch!' he cries.

I run towards him, holding him back with what little strength is left in my weak body. The words are out of my mouth before I can even think them through. 'Nobody else has to get hurt today. Let him go, and we can call the police. They'll handle everything.'

'It's not something he should walk away from,' Freddy spits.

'Maybe not, but the law will take care of it.'

'Are you really going to be okay with him just being behind bars?'

'We don't have a choice.'

'That's not true. I could beat the bastard to death.'

'Just... don't.'

There's a resignation in my voice that seems to affect him somehow. It starts with the lowering of his fist. Then he lets go of Tony and turns, slowly, to face me. His twisted features soften, like he's just awoken from a nightmare and adjusted to the fact it was only a dream. A really long, horrible dream that will stay with him forever.

I glance down at Tony. He's on his back in the grass, his chest bobbing up and down as he mourns. Then I meet Freddy's eye. 'As much as I want to take some anger out on him, there's been enough of that. He's just lost his son. Even if Cillian was a piece of shit, Tony is suffering enough. Think about it: you can take his phone – he probably has it on him – call the fire brigade and the police, and that will take care of both me and him.'

Freddy's jaw grinds from side to side. He lowers his gaze.

'You know you'll go to prison, too.'

'Can you live with that?'

'It might not be punishment enough.'

'Then do the other thing.'

I swallow hard because 'the other thing' means the end of the road for me. Freddy wants revenge for his brother, and I won't fight him on it. It's just a sad, melancholy acknowledgement of all the wrong I've done. As long as Tony doesn't have to suffer any more than he already is, I couldn't care less what happens to me. Even if the thought is terrifying.

After a long, uncomfortable silence, Freddy turns to look down at the old man. There's no telling what he'll do – how he'll adjust to the situation with so much hate in his heart. Then, surprising us both, he kneels in front of Tony and speaks.

'Give me your phone.'

———

LIGHTS FLASH IN THE DISTANCE. Multiple. The fire brigade and the police are all on their way, but they're going to need a lot more than that once they see the mess we've all made of the once beautiful home on the hill. It's all I can do to stand here and stare at my impending doom.

'I'm tempted to leave you here,' Freddy says, Tony still sobbing at his feet.

'You can do whatever you feel is necessary.' I look him in the eye to demonstrate my sincerity. 'I meant what I said. About being done running. About how I'm ready to take responsibility for my actions. Would it make you feel better to kill me?'

'It's hard to say.'

'There isn't much time left to decide.'

'Yeah, no shit.'

The lights grow stronger as they speed along the distance, travelling up the only road to this mess. It's a bizarre feeling, watching your future travel towards you but also knowing you could be dead before they reach you. If Freddy is going to go through with it, he'll have to do it fast. As in under-a-minute fast. I wonder how he would do it. Would he strangle me? Strike me with the crowbar? It's not in his hand – who knows where he dropped it.

'Does anyone know you were here?' Freddy asks.

'What?'

He takes me by the arm, leads me away from Tony. Just enough to be out of earshot. Then his voice simmers to a mumble. 'Cillian took you from the clinic, but did anyone see you leave? I'm guessing not, considering you've been trapped here.'

'No, I... don't think so.'

'And nobody came or went?'

'Only those who were dismissed or killed.'

'But did they know your name?'

'No. Why?'

Freddy nods like he's just figured it all out. Then he returns to Tony and drops to a knee. 'What's this woman's name?' he asks, jerking a pointed finger into his chest as if to snap him from his misery. 'Look at me. What. Is. Her. Name?'

'I—I don't know,' Tony says, wiping away his tears. 'She never said.'

'What do you know about her?'

'What? Only that my son knew her.'

'Did he say *how* he knew her?'

'No. For all I know, they've been friends for years or just days.'

Freddy turns to me, and I know what he's thinking. There is no trail linking me to Cillian. The surgical team don't know I went home with Cillian. Manuel and Isabella couldn't give out my name even if they were here. Even Tony has no idea who I am, and I don't remember them taking before and after pictures. Between all of this and the fact that Freddy came here on his own, there is absolutely no way to find out who we are.

It's like we were just faces.

'Let me make one thing clear,' Freddy says, grabbing Tony by the throat. 'The only reason I'm leaving you to the police is because I feel sorry for you. Two innocent people were trapped in the cellar by your headcase of a son, and you did nothing to get us out of there. Nothing whatsoever. So I may be sparing your life, but you don't deserve it.'

Freddy stands and faces me one last time. 'We're leaving.'

'We are?' Relief breezes through me. 'But so we're clear...'

'I don't know what to do with you, but we're not staying here.'

'That sounds fair.'

We wait just long enough for the police to arrive, and then we start backing away. There are some trees not far from us, and that's the only place we can run to. When the authorities are close enough, the fields flashing red and blue, we finally run to a safe distance and leave Tony behind. I have no idea if he was lying about us – if he might know more than he's letting on – but we're going to have to trust him, even if just a little.

As we flee, however, one final thought occurs to me. I stop dead, and Freddy lingers just long enough to shout at me. He tells me to hurry up, or he'll just have to leave me. The police are close – too close – but I just might have enough time. I decide to risk it, run back, and say one last thing to Tony while he cries for Cillian.

'I'm sorry about your son.'

Then, vanishing into darkness, I join Freddy on the run.

WE EMERGE on the hill overlooking the house. Standing side by side, we watch the fire blaze on and the men using their equipment to fight it. It's hard to make out everything, but the flashes of emergency lights and the glow from the flames helps illuminate the darkness.

'We almost died in there,' Freddy says.

'Someone actually did.'

I think back to Cillian and how his final act was attempted murder. I'll never forget the image of him lurking above me with the fire extinguisher held high above his head. Then the sound – that awful sound as the crowbar struck his skull. I don't want to believe that Freddy was the man who killed him. I try telling myself it was the fire.

That's the best way to think of it.

'You actually feel sorry for him, don't you?'

'Who?' I ask. 'Cillian?'

'No, his dad.'

'A little.'

'Try to remember he did nothing to help us.'

'Yeah, but maybe he's not all bad.'

'Well, it's not like we'll ever know.'

Another silence. This one longer, both of us

staring as Tony is checked over by a paramedic. I can't see his expression from here, but my mind is filling in the blanks and making me hear his awful, heartbreaking cries all over again. I shouldn't be staring, but if I ever stop, then it will be time to get down to business – time for Freddy to do what we've been waiting for. I'm starting to think it will be easier to deal with death than the anxiety of waiting for it.

'What now?' I ask. 'With you and me, I mean.'

'Not like I can kill you here and now, is it?'

'But you're going to. Eventually.' It's not a question.

'Let's just get tonight over with.'

'Whatever that means.'

Freddy is gone before I can say any more. I follow him down the other side of the hill, where his Jeep is sitting between some trees and waiting for us. I get in without questioning my safety because it's this or turning myself in.

So we just drive, headlights off until we get far, far away from the scene of the crime. Then the beams come on, and we still sit in silence. It's processing time for Freddy, I'm sure, and it gives me a chance to think about Cillian. That man was such a mess – a *mean* mess – and a lot of that was probably attributed to a bunch of mental health problems. How much of it was his fault? How much was he really in control?

All I know is I'm lucky to be alive.

It's funny, I never would've made it out if it weren't for the man who'd come to kill me. Now, we're sitting side by side as we flee the place we were trapped in, and all I can think about is how sorry I feel for Tony. For Cillian, too, which is weird but will probably make more sense to me in time. For now, I'll just have to put this behind me and carry on with my life.

However much of it is left, that is.

Chapter 32
Daisy, Now

Freddy never did take my life.

I wait for it every day, certain it will happen at some point. Until then, he's living his life, and I'm living mine, although he does drop in at least once a day. It's usually to remind me that this peace won't last forever and that he's still struggling to come to terms with what happened back at Cillian's house. Or, I suppose... Tony's house.

Speaking of Tony, he's disappeared after being questioned by the police for Isabella's murder. Her body was found in the woods near his home. It's all over the news – he got out of the police station and was last seen on airport security cameras, where records show he then took a trip to somewhere in the United States. I have a feeling that's the last

The Plastic Surgeon

we'll be seeing of him. Bizarre though it may sound, I wish him luck.

I know how it feels to lose someone.

It's been five days since we got away from that house, and nobody has come for us. I keep expecting the police to turn up at my door, if not for that, then at least in connection with Jason's murder. It was important to Freddy that his brother got a proper burial, so he made an anonymous tip to the police that the body was in the woods, and that's started its own line of questioning. The police just left my house, actually, and my tears were real... but I think they bought my performance when I denied all knowledge of his death.

I have a feeling they'll be back though.

It's actually scary that Freddy hasn't dropped my name to them. It now feels real that he intends to do something about me – to get the revenge he wanted. Why else would you keep a secret like that away from the authorities? Because of that – and also to hide from the curious looks my neighbours give me – I stay inside most of the day, trying to make the house feel like my own home rather than the one I shared with my late husband.

I've heard from Lily, too. She says Freddy called her and said not to bother picking me up from the clinic, then apologised profusely for causing me any trouble. It's a good thing she's so concerned about having upset me, as it distracts her from the details of my whereabouts. I wonder how long it will take for someone to piece all of this together: Jason's murder, my disappearance, the burning of the White estate, and whatever happens to me next.

Only Freddy knows what will happen after I'm gone. This morning, he lets himself in using his brother's key that he refuses to return. I'm in the middle of washing the dishes, and he stands in the doorway with his arms folded, staring me down.

I've never seen such hate.

'You don't have to drop by just to remind me I'm a bitch,' I tell him.

'Well, I didn't know what else to do. I'm going crazy at home alone.'

'So what do you want from me? Another apology?'

'Company.'

Our eyes lock, and it's uncomfortable for about five seconds before I open my mouth. I had every intention of telling him to leave, but instead, a serious question that's been haunting me falls from my lips. 'When are you going to get it over with?'

'Soon.'

'Why not now?'

Freddy shrugs. 'Suspicion, I guess. People will start asking questions, and I haven't even processed any of this. Let's get my brother's funeral out of the way, and maybe then we can look at the best way to punish you for what you did.'

'Sure. Can't wait.'

'Don't be sarcastic. It's for the weak.'

'Perhaps I'm just weak.'

'Perhaps.'

Without another word, Freddy goes into the living room and sits in his brother's chair. The TV comes on, and some crappy quiz show starts blaring louder than I'm comfortable with. I should feel at ease knowing I've got a few more days to live – Jason's funeral is just around the corner, and we're going to give him the send-off he deserves. After that, who even knows what's going to happen to me?

All I know is it won't be pretty.

JASON'S FUNERAL is a quiet affair on a wet and breezy morning. Some people look at me, probably thinking it's weird that I can't seem to get out a tear, but they offer their condolences the whole time. It's nice knowing they're here for me, but the looks of utter disgust I keep getting from Freddy make me uncomfortable. I've never been this anxious before.

It's because I might be dead tomorrow.

After the funeral, we all go to Jason's favourite pub to share stories about his life. So many people touch me on the shoulder, putting drinks in front of me and asking if I'm okay. The truth is, I'm a million miles from okay. It's not that I'm torn apart by my husband's death, but the fact I'm more concerned for my own coming murder that riddles me with guilt. I've proven time and time again how selfish I can be – how desperate I am to put my own needs above anyone else's – and the fact I can't cry at my own husband's funeral says it all.

I really am a disgusting human being.

After the wake, when everyone has said their goodbyes, Freddy takes me home and tells me to go inside. It's perfectly natural for guilt to overrule my grief, so I sit beside him in the Jeep for a while before saying anything. It's because there's nothing left to say. The apologies are running dry, and the only remaining question is something I don't want to have answered.

I just wish he'd get it over with.

'Are you going inside or not?' he asks, tiredness reddening his eyes. Could be the tears.

'Eventually. It's just facing that house, you know? Everything inside has something to do with him – something he owned, built, or destroyed. There's a different memory in every room, and the kitchen is the worst of them all.'

'You've brought this on yourself.'

'Yeah, you don't need to remind me,' I huff. 'Tonight is just different. Maybe it's the funeral, all those memories coming back. Different memories. Good ones. I know you're not interested in hearing it, but I just... don't want to go home.'

Freddy sighs. Then, after a few seconds of awkward silence, he shoves down the handbrake, shifts the gearstick, and accelerates down the road. I don't need to ask where we're going, and he doesn't bother to tell me. It's obvious.

We're going back to his house.

To say it feels weird under his roof is an understatement, but I'm impressed by his ability to still show me basic human kindness. Freddy sets me up in his bed and insists he'll take the sofa. It's perfectly okay that he hurls the extra pillows at me, saying very little except for when he has to tell me something about the hallway lights being on a sensor or the bathroom flush getting stuck. I'm not really listening because all I can think about is saying sorry. No amount of apologies will ever be enough, but I'll keep trying.

'I'm so, so sorry,' I tell him before he leaves.

'Don't,' he says, his back to me in the doorway.

'I feel it, so I'm saying it.'

'But I don't want to talk about it.'

'You don't have to. Just know that I don't blame you for hating me.'

Freddy closes the door and leaves without saying goodnight. I lie there in the dark, thinking only of my dead husband and how this whole thing is all my fault. I owe Freddy a debt I can never repay, and to make things worse, he's treating me like a friend by letting me stay in his house. In his *bed*. It even smells like Jason. Is that even possible?

I don't know how much time goes by, but the pillow is soaked in my tears. My chest is all clogged up with heartache, and it hurts. I wish my husband was here to calm and soothe me. But the visitor who slowly opens the door isn't Jason.

It's his brother.

Somehow, I know what he wants. It's not to kill me like he keeps promising. Some strange kind of bond has formed between us since the night Cillian died, and we're both too stubborn to admit it. Him because he hates me, and me because it's a betrayal to my husband.

Yet, I can't deny what I'm feeling.

Freddy slips off his shirt and slides into bed beside me. We don't talk – he just holds me close to his chest. It takes three seconds before we start kissing, and moments later, he's inside me. It's hard, rough, and exciting, but also completely natural. It's one of the best experiences of my life, but he just can't seem to hide the grudge he's holding back. It's present in his every move – every firm grip on my skin that pulls just a little too tight.

Afterwards, unlike other men who get what they want, he stays and lets me sleep on his chest. Do I trust him not to cut my throat in the night? Not really, and I wouldn't blame him if he did, but at least I'll sleep right through it. At least, I hope so.

I'm still crying until there are no tears left. Now I have guilt to throw into the mix, I just don't know how to get by. Maybe it's a good thing Freddy wants me dead. It will be a better world without me, so the sooner he does it, the better.

I think I'm ready.

———

WE SPEND all of the next day together. It's not awkward like it should be – we basically coexist, lounging around at home as if this is the start of a whole new life. The problem is, I don't trust him in this quiet state. Freddy seems too cold. Too calculating.

I don't like it one bit.

Throughout the day, while he slowly throws together bits for lunch, he can't stay away from the whisky. It's not hard to understand why – his brother was buried yesterday, and he spent last night with the man's wife. Hence, the disdain when he looks at me.

Hence, the deep sigh when he sits nearby.

'We need to talk,' he says.

'Yes, we do.'

I know what's coming. There's not a hope in hell that he can live with the regret of what he's done. Not without taking his revenge on the woman who killed his brother. I sit there in shame, squeezing my own fingers to avoid contact while I wait for my demise.

'I've always loved you,' he says.

My head shoots up. 'What?'

'It's not a new feeling. I've loved you from the minute we met. Do I hate you for what you did? Of course, but I could never bring myself to kill you. Quite the opposite, actually. Because we're going through grief together. Obviously, you feel something for me too, and that doesn't mean we have to rush it, but—'

'Stop,' I tell him.

'You can't deny our—'

'No. You don't understand.'

'I do. Let me explain myself.'

'Please...'

'I'm trying to tell you how much I want to be with—'

'Freddy, we need to get you to a hospital!'

It's entirely my fault, but there's a fair explanation. I truly believed Freddy would want to kill me today. There wasn't an ounce of doubt that this was my last day on earth. I never in a million years expected him to confess his love for me.

That's why I put the poison in his drink.

To get him before he gets me.

He knows it now, after he takes another sip. It has a different kick to it. Something clinical, perhaps synthetic. The burn shows on his twisted expression, like lava is spilling into the pit of his stomach. He whines as it falls down his neck. Or maybe that's his throat, a plea for help drowned out by the gargling sound that follows.

'Help' is what it sounds like.

For all the good it does. The only person in the room is the one who's done this to him – me. Freddy stumbles back, reaching for his throat as if it will help. It won't – nothing will. This man is as good as dead, and he knows it. How can he not?

His back strikes the wall with a violent crash. He doubles over, then begins to pace as his vision grows blurry. I panic and shoot to my feet, reaching into my pocket for a phone that isn't there. Tears sting my eyes as I watch another man die because of me.

He runs for the front door, reaching for the handle to get far away. His hand hits flat air twice before finding purchase. Then, while he tries to make it to the end of the gravel driveway, his legs give out. The ground rushes up to meet him, and he does nothing.

Nothing.

Freddy's eyes flutter and then close. There's no way he's getting up from this – no way he will live to see another day. This is the end of his journey, and all I can think about is how I'll have to live with this regret for the rest of my life. No amount of running will ever fill this burning hole of self-loathing. No amount of surgery will make my inner self beautiful.

Just like his brother, Freddy's dead.

Just like his brother, it's my fault.

How can I ever go on?

For other books by AJ Carter, visit:

www.ajcarterbooks.com/books

About the Author

AJ Carter is a psychological thriller author from Bristol, England. His first book, *The Family Secret*, is praised by critics around the world, and he continues to regularly deliver suspenseful novels you can't put down.

Sign up to his mailing list today and be the first to hear about upcoming releases and hot new deals for existing books. You'll also receive a FREE digital copy of *The Couple Downstairs* – an unputdownable domestic thriller you won't find anywhere else in the world.

www.ajcarterbooks.com/subscribe

Made in United States
Orlando, FL
27 September 2024

52022925R00203